A
BRANDONBURG
Christmas

Thanks

Enjoy + God Bless

Ross

Thanks!

Enjoy + God bless

Ross

A BRANDONBURG
Christmas

written by Ross Adams

TATE PUBLISHING & *Enterprises*

Published by Tate Publishing & Enterprises, LLC
127 E. Trade Center Terrace | Mustang, Oklahoma 73064 USA
1.888.361.9473 | www.tatepublishing.com

Tate Publishing is committed to excellence in the publishing industry. The company reflects the philosophy established by the founders, based on Psalm 68:11,
"The Lord gave the word and great was the company of those who published it."

Book design copyright © 2011 by Tate Publishing, LLC. All rights reserved.
Cover and interior design by Scott Parrish
Illustrations by Kathy Hoyt

Published in the United States of America

ISBN: 978-1-61777-293-1
1. Juvenile Fiction / Holidays & Celebrations / Christmas & Advent
2. Juvenile Fiction / Religious / Christian / Friendship
11.11.08

INTRODUCTION
To the readers of this book:

A Brandonburg Christmas is a work for all ages and can be read by anyone, anywhere, at any time, but my intent in writing it was specific: a read aloud book. My prayer is that it be read out loud, by parents to their children on the days leading up to Christmas.

Many large words and complex phrases have been left in by design to motivate the child to ask questions therefore prompting the parent to either explain it or look it up if they aren't sure. This in turn promotes communication in the areas of conversation and learning for both parent and child. Joey's character is intended to be inspirational and reveal the power of God in his life. The purpose of this book is to entertain and teach. I want it to portray real life yet press beyond the natural to the supernatural. It is meant to promote spending time with your children and focusing on the positive, even as you deal with the negative. I hope that it will inspire the listener and the reader to pray at night and talk to God throughout the day; help them to focus on family yet defer to helping others; celebrate Christmas but still draw them to its true meaning; tell a familiar story but add a fresh perspective.

Day 1:
Saturday, December 21

It was Saturday afternoon and quite cool, but that wasn't unusual for Vermont in December. The three young boys playing ball in the vacant lot on Mill Street didn't even notice as the water in Mr. Baker's drainage spout formed stalactite-like ice formations into the catch pail. They were far too busy to be bothered by a little cold weather.

"Here, runt, catch this one!" yelled Bobby as he lofted the ball high over Joey's head. Bobby called him "runt" because he was so much smaller than the rest of the boys. Joey didn't mind, though. He knew that it wasn't how big you were on the outside that mattered. It was how big you were on the inside; and every time Bobby called him "runt," he got a little bit bigger.

"That's too high!" yelled Joey as he jumped for the ball.

"Go get it, Joey," Michael demanded. "You're the one who missed it, so you're the one who has to chase it." Joey shrugged and headed after the ball. When he looked up to see where it was going, he noticed an old man crossing directly into its path.

"Watch out!" hollered Joey. But before the old man knew what was happening, the ball struck him squarely on the leg, forcing him to lose his balance and fall abruptly to the ground.

"I'm sorry, sir. Are you all right?" Joey asked.

The old man looked up at the young boy with a stern look on his face and tried to erect himself. "I'm perfectly fine, you little urchin," he snapped. "If I am not, your parents will hear from my attorney."

The young boy picked up his ball, then turned to the old man and flashed an innocent yet caring smile.

"I truly am sorry, sir." Noticing that the old man was having trouble getting to his feet, Joey offered his assistance. "Can I help?"

"I need no one's help!" the old man responded. Seeing his hat on the ground next to him, he reached down, picked it up, brushed the snow off, and then turned his attention back to Joey. "If you want to help, get out my way." The old man made his way to his feet, while Joey stood watching. "Now be gone, before I call a patrolman."

Joey turned to go and then stopped. "I do hope you're all right. Have a good day, sir."

"A good day, indeed," grumbled the old man as he continued on his way.

As Joey neared the other boys, he heard them talking about the old man.

"What a mean old coot."

"That's old man Brandon. He lives in that big house on the hill. He doesn't like people, only money."

"Yeah, he probably wants to marry it." Bobby and Michael laughed.

"I think he's probably nice," Joey said.

"No way. He's the meanest man in the whole world."

"Yeah, he yelled at you just for trying to get the ball," added Michael.

"You don't even know him. You shouldn't talk bad about people if you don't know them."

"We know you. You're a dummy."

"No, I'm not."

"Yes, you are. You think old man Brandon is nice when he's really mean," Bobby taunted.

"I think you guys are mean. He could have gotten hurt. Here, take this dumb ole ball." Joey threw the ball to Bobby. "I don't want to play anymore." With that, he turned and walked away.

"Good-bye, runt!" Bobby yelled after him. "What a baby."

"Yeah, what a baby," Michael echoed.

Meanwhile, Nicholas Brandon had made his way to the bottom of a long driveway that wound its way up a rather steep hill and finally ended at the porch entrance of a huge mansion. He was resting in preparation for the strenuous walk to the top of the drive. With a deep breath, he started up the hill. Just as Nicholas reached the halfway point of his climb, Joey appeared at the base of the hill. He watched as the old man slowly ascended. Once Nicholas was up the hill and inside the house, Joey quickly followed. Finding a small window on the lower level of the house, he peered inside. He found himself looking into what appeared to be a large den. On one side of the room, there was a huge Victorian desk and chair set with a whole wall full of books behind it. On the other side of the room was a large fireplace with a giant marble mantle filled with various trinkets. In front of the fireplace lay a beautiful Oriental rug, and on top of the rug was a big cushioned chair and a coffee table that looked like it had once been a tree stump.

Just in front of the coffee table was the biggest dog that Joey had ever seen. At first, he thought it was a horse but soon came to his senses, realizing that horses rarely live indoors. It was in actuality a Belgian wolfhound. Suddenly, the door to the room opened and Nicholas entered. He was carrying a big plate of meat scraps, which he laid on the floor in front of the dog. The old man gently patted his companion's head and sat down in the cushioned chair as the cream-colored canine calmly began to eat. After finishing half of the meat on the plate, the dog walked over to the chair and licked the old man's hand. Nicholas bent down and smiled at the dog, lovingly stroking his soft white hair, then kissed him on the nose. Seeing this, Joey was proud of himself for being right about the old man. Satisfied, he headed for home.

When Joey arrived home it was already dark. Upon entering the house, he saw his mother in the kitchen.

"Joey? Is that you? You're late, dear. Where have you been?"

"I was playing ball with Bobby and Michael. I took the long way home."

"You know you're supposed to be in by dark."

"Yeah, I know, Mom. I'm sorry. It won't happen again. I promise."

"That's all right. Now go and get ready for dinner."

Joey went to the bathroom and washed his hands and face. By the time he returned to the dining room, his mother already had dinner on the table.

"Chicken and dumplings, my favorite!" he shouted. Joey loved chicken and dumplings more than … well … anything, except maybe flapjacks. His mom spooned a large helping of the delicious hot dish onto his plate as Joey waited anxiously. Then it happened—vegetables. As his father lifted the lid, Joey's worst dinner fear came true: *spinach*. Joey hated spinach more than … well … anything, except maybe broccoli.

"You eat your vegetables, son, they're good for you. Make you grow up big and strong." That was the cruelest thing Joey's father could have possibly said. "I want your plate cleaned, or you won't be getting any pie for dessert." Make that the second cruelest thing. Joey went right to work on the chicken and dumplings. He didn't pay a lot of attention to dinner conversation when his most favorite food in the whole wide world was in front of him. But, as it must be, all good things come to an end. The chicken and dumplings part of dinner was gone and now it was time for vegetables. Suddenly, talk around the table became eminently important.

"They say we may have to close the mill down if we can't get some new equipment." It was his father's voice, and it had a sincere tone that Joey only heard when something bad was about to happen.

"You mean that they'll have to lay everyone off?" Mother responded. "Why don't they just get the stuff they need and get on with it?"

"There's no money. The equipment is very expensive, but without it, it's just too dangerous.""What are we going to do? Christmas is in four days. How will we make it through the winter?"

"We'll do what we always do, make the best of it. We have some necessities stored away. We'll be all right. But I'm a little worried about some of the other guys at work. They have much larger families than ours and aren't as well prepared."

"Everything will be all right, Dad. They'll get the money somehow," Joey piped in pleasantly.

"Thanks, Joey. You're right. It's going to be just fine. That's a good lesson for us to learn. If we're going to expect miracles, we better start by believing in them and then speaking them into existence. Mother, how about a piece of pie for this young man?"

"Even though I haven't finished my *spinach* yet?"

"We'll make an exception this time."

"Oh, boy!" Feeling obligated, Joey finished his vegetables anyway, and then he ate his pie.

After dinner, he brushed his teeth and put on his pajamas. Then his dad read to him from the Bible. It was the part about the birth of Jesus. After a while, Joey could feel the little sleep crystals forming at the corners of his eyes. Dad's chin was getting closer and closer to his chest with each page he read. Joey could have sworn that he was actually reading with his eyes closed for a while. Soon, the story was over. It was bedtime. Joey's mom tucked him in and kissed him goodnight. As Joey closed his eyes, he said his prayers.

"Dear Jesus, I hope you get lots of presents on your birthday. I pray for Daddy's work to get new equipment so he can keep his job. I pray for Grandma and Grandpa, and Mommy and Daddy, and all my friends. I also pray for Mr. Brandon, 'cause he's not really mean AMEN!"

DAY 2:
Sunday, December 22

The sun was shining through the drapes in Joey's room at such an angle that the one beam of light that had fought its way through just happened to be right in Joey's eyes. He thought he was dreaming about summer again when he heard his mother's voice from downstairs.

"Joey, get up. It's time for church. And don't forget your winter coat." Joey opened his eyes, and *wow*, that was no dream. It was the sun, and boy was it real. Now Joey understood why his father had always told him not to look directly into the sun, because when you did, you couldn't see for about a hundred years. As soon as he regained his sight, Joey got up and put on his

Sunday best. He liked getting dressed up. It made him feel important. He could pretend he was a prominent businessman getting ready to make a big deal. Then he could save Dad's mill from closing down. Even if he didn't know anybody who had money, except old man Brandon, and he didn't really know him, it was fun to pretend. Joey picked up his winter coat and trotted downstairs. When he reached the foot of the stairs, he smelled it. Sunday breakfast was the best meal of the week. Mom always made eggs and bacon and, you guessed it, flapjacks. Last night chicken and dumplings; this morning flapjacks. Wasn't life grand? Joey wolfed down his breakfast, and soon they were off to church.

In the sermon, Joey heard the same story his father had read to him the night before. All about how Mary and Joseph had come to Bethlehem, only to find that the inn was full. So they had to sleep in a stable with all the animals. How Jesus had been born and put in a manger. About the bright star that showed the way. How the three wise men traveled from far, far away just to see the newborn King and bring him gifts. There was also a little boy there who played his drum, at least that was what one of the songs said. There was something different in the story the preacher told though, something that Joey couldn't quite comprehend. The preacher talked about how Jesus was born so he could die and make the world a better place for those who lived. Then there was a bunch more singing and praying and other stuff. After all, a seven-year-old boy's attention span is only so long.

Soon church was over. In the fellowship room, Joey saw Bobby and Michael. He told them about Nicholas and the big dog, and how Nicholas had been so kind and loving with the dog that he couldn't possibly be mean. But Bobby and Michael didn't believe him; they called him a liar and said he had made it up just so he could be right.

"No, I didn't," said Joey. "If you don't believe me, you can go and see for yourself."

"Okay, we will," Bobby and Michael responded in unison. The boys decided to meet at the playground, then go to old man Brandon's place from there.

At one o'clock the three boys met at the playground. They discussed the plan, and then headed for the Brandon mansion. They made their way up the hill to the little window where Joey had been not twenty-four hours earlier. When they looked inside, no one was there. No big white dog lying on the Oriental rug, no plate full of meat scraps, no old man sitting in a cushioned chair laughing and playing. Just a lifeless room.

"I knew you were lying," Bobby chided.

"I'm not lying. There was a dog, and Mr. Brandon was nice to him."

"Oh, yeah," mocked Michael. "I'll prove it." Michael banged sharply on the glass as the three boys peered through. Suddenly, from beneath the window, Caesar, the huge white wolfhound, jumped into full view. The only thing the boys could see was a mass of white with the biggest, sharpest teeth since Tyrannosaurus Rex bared right in their faces. Bobby stumbled backwards, knocking Michael into Joey, who fell into a small snowdrift. The boys scrambled to their feet and sprinted back down the hill. Joey, being smaller than the other two, was beginning to fall behind when the front door opened.

"Run faster, Joey!" yelled Bobby.

"I'm trying!"

From behind him, Joey heard the deep bellowing sound of what had to be the largest animal without antlers he had ever seen. It was Caesar, and he was gaining rapidly.

"You've got to run faster, Joey!" shouted Michael, who was now thirty or forty feet ahead.

"I can't…" just as Joey spoke he stepped into a deep patch in the snow and fell flat on his stomach. Bobby and Michael stopped momentarily to look back at their helpless comrade.

"Should we go and get help?" asked Michael.

"Maybe…I don't know…No! We'll get in big trouble if someone finds out we were sneaking around up here," decided Bobby. The duo continued on.

Joey had turned over and was trying to get back to his feet when Caesar jumped him. Silent with fear, he looked back to see his two best friends lumbering through the snow like a couple of wounded elk, and then out of sight. In the meantime, Caesar had Joey pinned to the ground and was hovering over him. Joey's mind raced with the thought of everything he had done wrong in the last year. How could he say he was sorry? How could he make it up to everyone? Just then he felt the hot breath of the dog on his neck. This was it. He was done for. Caesar opened his huge mouth, his teeth moving ever closer to the young boy's throat. With a sudden jerk of Caesar's head, Joey felt the animal's huge tongue slap him alongside of the face over and over again, until Joey's silence turned to uncontrolled laughter, as the gentle giant smothered him with affection.

"Caesar! Come here. Caesar! Leave the poor child alone." As Caesar backed away, Nicholas appeared at Joey's side with a large blanket.

"Are you all right?" inquired the old man.

"Yes. I'm fine. Thank you."

"You know, it's against the law to go on people's property without permission. It's called trespassing."

"Yes, I know," Joey confessed. "I just wanted to show them that you were nice. They said you were mean and didn't like people, only money. But I saw you with your dog and you kissed him and gave him a big plate of meat. You're not really mean, are you?"

"You better come inside and get those wet clothes off. You can sit by the fire until they dry." He wrapped the blanket around the frozen youth and led him into the house. Once inside, Nicholas set Joey's clothes out in front of the fireplace to dry. Joey sat in the big cushioned

chair, wrapped snugly in the blanket that Nicholas had brought him. He scanned the room, his eyes darting from object to object. He had a strange feeling about this place. It was like being locked in a toy store after hours, so many things to see, but afraid to touch. While taking inventory of the room's contents, Joey's eyes settled on the mantle full of trinkets and locked on one particularly interesting piece of memorabilia. It was a small gold coin. It wasn't terribly shiny or extraordinarily beautiful to look at, but there was something about it that sparked Joey's interest. The way it sat up there among all those other articles of nostalgia and yet somehow stood alone. Joey had just climbed out of the huge chair and shuffled over to get a better look when Nicholas and Caesar entered.

"Here's your hot chocolate, young man.," Nicholas announced. "By the way, I didn't get your name."

"Joey, sir." Nicholas handed him the steaming brew as he turned away from the mantle. "Thank you," he said.

"I'm—"

"Nicholas Brandon," Joey interrupted.

"That's correct. What is it that you find so interesting?" the old man queried.

"It's that old coin in the purple box."

"That was the first coin that my grandfather ever earned. He gave it to my father and then he gave it to me. It doesn't shine like it used to. It's been sitting on that mantle for years."

"I think it's wonderful," gasped Joey. As he returned to the cushioned chair and took a sip of his hot chocolate, Caesar came over and licked his hand then lay down at his feet.

"He likes you. Any friend of Caesar's is a friend of mine," stated Nicholas.

"Why did you name him Caesar?" asked Joey.

"I didn't. A friend of mine brought him to me. Caesar was just a puppy then. My friend said, 'Nicky, I'd like you to meet Caesar. Take good care of him.' I'm not sure if he was talking to me or the dog, but he's been my best friend ever since."

The old man and the young boy talked for a long time. Joey had so many questions and Nick had all the answers. *It's nice to have someone to talk to who actually talks back,* Nicholas thought as the conversation continued. They talked about how Nicholas's grandfather had started the town from a small mine over 150 years ago.

"I'm the only Brandon left," Nicholas said.

"Didn't you ever get married?" Joey asked.

"Yes. I was married once, to a wonderful woman. We were very happy, until one winter she caught pneumonia and passed away. We never had any children. That's when I started spending my time alone here with Caesar. The kids think I'm pretty mean because I never talk to anyone. I guess I just got used to being alone."

"You mean you don't have any family at all?" Joey exclaimed.

"Just Caesar," the old man replied.

"I don't know what I'd do without my mom and dad, and all of our family and friends," said Joey. "I'm so sorry. I think I understand why you act the way you do now." As the conversation went on, they talked about Joey's dad and how the mill might have to close down if they couldn't get some new equipment. "Then my dad would lose his job as foreman and lots of his friends would lose their jobs, too," Joey said.

"I'm confident everything will work out just fine," said Nicholas.

"It's starting to get dark. I don't really want to, but I'd better get going. I promised my mom that I wouldn't be late anymore," Joey admitted. Nicholas gathered Joey's clothes and handed them to him. He quickly put them on and headed for the door, only to be cut off at the pass by Caesar.

"Caesar, get out of my way. I have to go home. I'm going to be late," Joey pleaded.

"Caesar, move from the young man's path. A boy's promise to his mother is a sacred vow, not to be interrupted by man or beast. Joey will come and visit again." With this, the cordial canine moved aside, and Joey opened the door.

"Can I really come and visit again, Nicholas?"

"I'm counting on it. I need someone to polish that old coin. I mean, if you're interested. I take Caesar for his walk every morning bright and early if you'd like to come along."

"Sure thing, I'll be back tomorrow."

"Very well then. Say good-bye, Caesar." Caesar gave a loud "woof," and Joey exited.

It had been a long day for Nicholas, and he was very tired. He made his way back to the cushioned chair and sat down. Then he picked up the telephone receiver and rang a number.

"Hello Erik, I'd like to speak with you tomorrow morning. I have some very important matters I'd like to discuss." Then, he hung up the receiver and leaned back in his chair. As he relaxed, a coughing fit overtook him. Nicholas pulled out his handkerchief and coughed into it. Looking down at the silky white cloth in his hand, he saw the same thing he'd been seeing for the last two months—blood. Caesar walked over to his friend, licked him lovingly on the cheek, and lay down on the floor at his feet. Soon, man and beast were fast asleep.

Back at home, Joey arrived only minutes before dusk. When he walked through the door, his father had just finished putting a large Christmas tree into its stand and was about to start decorating.

"Can I help?" were the first words out of Joey's mouth.

"What? No 'Hello, how do you do?' Just, 'can I help?'" Father quoted playfully. "Of course you can help. You didn't think we were going to do it by ourselves, did you? Go over there and get me that popcorn string and box of ornaments." For the better part of the next hour, Joey and his family debated, experimented, and discussed the plan; carefully placing each ornament in just the right spot, until the tree was perfect. For the finishing touch, Joey's dad lifted him up onto his shoulders so he could put the handmade angel on top, the one his grandmother had made from an old corn husk and a walnut shell.

"Have you ever seen such a beautiful tree?" Joey's mother exclaimed.

"It's perfect," announced Joey. "Is it time for dinner now?"

"That's our boy," quipped Father as they all headed into the kitchen.

After dinner, Dad was again lamenting the prospect of the mill closing, and Joey was once more giving his optimistic vision of the future. Joey had been debating whether or not to tell his parents about Nicholas. He had come to the conclusion that they should be told and figured that now was as good a time as any.

"I made a new friend today," he boldly proclaimed.

"I was wondering where you spent your day," his mother replied. "Bobby and Michael came over earlier and they seemed a little upset that you weren't home yet."

"I was at that big house on the hill."

"The old Brandon place?" questioned his father. "What were you doing there?"

"I was talking to Nicholas. He has a big dog named Caesar. He said I could come back tomorrow and polish his gold coin."

"Whoa, son. Nicholas? Gold coin? What exactly are you talking about?"

Joey told his mom and dad all about what had happened at the playground and how Bobby and Michael had made fun of Nicholas. How they had gone to the big house so he could show them that Nicholas wasn't mean. He told them about the gold coin and about how Nicholas didn't have any family now, except Caesar. And how Caesar liked him and any friend of Caesar's was a friend of Nicholas. He told them that he thought Nicholas was real nice and that an old man deserved to have friends, too.

"Is it okay if I go back there tomorrow? PLEASE!" Joey asked.

"I suppose it's all right, as long as you're not a bother," Mother cautioned.

"Oh, thank you, Mommy and Daddy. I won't be a bother. I promise."

"I'm sure you won't, son. Now go and get ready for bed."

"Okay, Dad. Goodnight. I love you, Mom and Dad." And off to bed he went.

"That is quite a boy." Dad beamed.

"He certainly is," Mom said as she nodded in agreement.

As Joey finished putting on his pajamas and climbed under the covers, his parents entered and crossed to his bed.

"Will I get lots of toys and things for Christmas?" Joey asked.

"You know, Joe, it's much better to give than to receive," Father responded.

"But how can I give somebody something if I don't have any money?"

"You make it with your own hands," his mother answered. "Something from the heart is much better than something from the store."

"Now quit worrying about Christmas presents and start worrying about sleep," warned Father. "Goodnight, son."

"Goodnight, Mom and Dad," said Joey as his parents closed the door behind them. Now it was time to talk to Jesus again.

"Dear Jesus, I pray for Daddy and Mommy and all my friends. I pray for Grandma and Grandpa and all the people in the world who don't have a Christmas tree. I pray for Nicholas, 'cause he's my friend and I love him, and I pray that I can make him something really special for Christmas. AMEN."

DAY 3:
Monday, December 23

The morning was crisp. The snow outside covered the ground like a fresh white pillowcase over one of Mother's fluffy goose-down pillows. The clouds were scattered across the sky with just a hint of sunshine behind them. It was going to be a wonderful day.

Joey was already dressed and in the kitchen looking for something to eat when his mother entered.

"Looking for something, dear?"

"I'm trying to find something to eat."

"If your stomach can wait five minutes, I'm making some oatmeal," his mother said cheerfully. "How about taking out the garbage while I get you a bowl?"

"Okay, Mom. But I'm kinda in a hurry. Could you make it real fast?"

"What's the big rush?" asked Mother as she stirred up the pot.

"I'm going to Nicholas's house. Remember?"

"Oh! That's right. Going to polish some coin or something. Are you sure Nicholas will be up yet?"

"Yeah, he gets up real early to take Caesar for a walk. He said if I get there in time, I can go with them. So I gotta hurry."

"You take out the garbage, and by the time you get back the oatmeal will be done."

"All right. Can I have some orange juice, too?"

"You sure can. Now you better get going."

Off went Joey, with garbage pail in hand, rushing to the rubbish pile like a fireman to a four alarm. When he returned, his mother had a hot bowl of oatmeal and a large glass of orange juice waiting for him. Joey finished his breakfast in about three minutes, then he grabbed his jacket, gave his mom a kiss, and he was gone. On his way, he made a little detour by the rubbish pile to pick up a big roast bone he'd noticed when he took out the garbage. He stashed the bone in his pocket and headed for Nicholas's.

The streets were busy with children playing and parents shopping for Christmas gifts. A spirit of peace had settled in on the little town. It was a special time, one that a seven-year-old boy in a hurry doesn't take time to acknowledge.

As Joey reached the top of the driveway, he noticed a tall man in a dark suit coming out of the house. He was carrying a black briefcase and had a strange look on his face. The tall man walked to his car, got in, and left. Joey moved slowly to the front door and knocked. Nicholas answered almost immediately with Caesar at his side.

"Good morning," Joey announced with a big grin on his face. "I'm here to polish the gold coin."

"That is fine. Shall we take Caesar for a walk first, though?" suggested Nicholas.

"Oh yes! I'd like that. But where do we walk?"

"Wherever Caesar wishes to go," said Nicholas playfully. Soon they were off; the old man, the young boy, and the dog. Through the snow, over the frozen pond, into the woods behind the great house, it was just as Nicholas had said.

Wherever Caesar wished to go. Finally, they returned to the warmth and comfort of the cozy den. Joey warmed his hands in front of the fireplace, while Nicholas fixed some more hot chocolate. Caesar curled up at the foot of the large cushioned chair, mauling Joey's roast bone the way a young boy might go after an ice cream cone on a hot summer day. After a couple of minutes, Nicholas returned with two cups of hot cocoa and a bowl of milk for Caesar.

"I can hardly wait. Is it time to polish the gold coin yet? " Joey asked as Nicholas handed him his mug.

"Whenever you're ready." The old man laughed. As Nicholas walked over and sat down next to Caesar, Joey pulled the tarnished trinket down from its place on the mantle. "There's some polish and a rag on the coffee table," said Nicholas. "I think you'll find them very useful."

And so the eager little boy set about his mission. Joey wasn't sure how long he'd been at work when he felt a wet tongue slop across the back of his neck. He looked up from his chore long enough to notice Nicholas asleep in the chair and Caesar circle the coffee table en route to his place at the foot of the dozing octogenarian. Joey finished up the final few spots he had left, placed the coin back in the purple box, and returned it to its rightful place among the plethora of memories, the kind that neither time nor age can erase. He found a pen and a scrap of paper on the tree stump table and scribbled a note. *I'm finished with the coin. I'll come back later to see you. Love, your friend Joey.* He started to leave, but when he reached the doorway he stopped. He turned around for one more look at the gold coin. He couldn't help but admire how it shined up there on that mantelpiece of life. He nodded in contentment and headed for home.

Joey could sense something even before he reached the front door, something different. He couldn't put his finger on it until he passed through the doorway and saw his father standing in the kitchen talking to his mother. He was using that tone again, only this time it was stronger. Something bad had happened. Upon entering the kitchen, he heard the story unfold.

" ... and he was just standing there when one of the cables snapped. I yelled 'Frank! Watch out!' but it was too late. The rod caught him flush, knocked him out cold. Doc says he has a severe concussion, could be brain damage. There's nothing I can do. I feel so helpless."

"I'm sure you did all you could do, dear," Mother comforted.

"Did something happen to Uncle Frank?" Joey asked. He wasn't really Joey's uncle, but he'd been Dad's best friend since Joey was born, so he seemed like an uncle.

"Yes, son. There was an accident at work today and he was hurt real bad." Dad continued on, laying out the details of the day's tragedy. "There's no way they can keep the mill open now," he concluded somberly.

"But Dad, they have to keep it open. How would anybody have Christmas?"

"Christmas isn't about money, Joe. It's about love and family. It's about Jesus and the way people feel at this time of year; the way that they care and give of themselves without thinking of the cost. The mill is something we don't have any control over, so we just have to take care of things as they happen, and so will everyone else. Do you understand what I'm saying, son?"

"I...I think so, Dad. You mean that we can only take care of what we do and we need to leave the rest up to God."

"Something like that, Joe. Something like that."

Joey's dad said something about going to the hospital to see Uncle Frank, but Joey didn't feel like going. Hospitals made him nervous. It might have been all the sick and hurt people with their families pacing around with worried looks on their faces. It might have been that the building was so big, and all the hallways looked the same. It might also be that it was just too clean there. Anyway, he had promised Nicholas that he would come back and see him later. He couldn't wait to see the look on Nicholas's face when he saw the way that gold coin shined. He was sure Nick would be proud of him.

"Mom and Dad, could I please go back to Nicholas's house? I promised him I would come back later to see him."

"Well, okay. But you have some lunch first and be home before dark," Mother warned.

"Oh, I will. I promise." With that, Joey rushed to the kitchen, ran to the cupboard, and pulled out the bread and the peanut butter. Then he was off to the refrigerator to get some of Mom's homemade strawberry jam. With his collection complete, he put together the best peanut butter and jam sandwich that the world had ever known. He kissed his mother good-bye and set out on his way. Walking to a friend's house seems a lot less time consuming when you are eating while you walk. As it turned out, Joey finished the walk and the sandwich at the same time; well, almost finished the walk and the sandwich. He still had the crusts left. He always peeled the crusts off his sandwiches. He wasn't that fond of the hard chewy outside; it was the soft tasty inside that he longed for. The part with good stuff on it. So, he hadn't officially finished the sandwich yet, and he still had that long, steep driveway to climb before he actually reached the house. But, other than that, the sandwich and the walk were finished at exactly the same time. Joey soon reached the front door, the one with the huge brass knocker. He had never noticed that knocker before. If he had, he also would have noticed how heavy it looked. He would have wondered how a boy such as himself might ever use it. It must have been seven feet high, which might as well be twenty when you're only three and a half feet tall. Luckily for Joey the doorbell was the same height as him, so he pushed it. Not long afterwards, he could hear the deep bellowing bark of Caesar getting closer and closer. Nicholas wasn't far behind and soon had the door open.

"Hello, young man. Come back to admire your work?"

"Do you like it? It wasn't even that hard to do. Actually, it was kinda fun. I think it looks wonderful. I hope you like it," Joey rambled as he secretly slipped Caesar the bread crusts from his sandwich.

"It looks great, Joey. Just great, better than it has in thirty years," Nicholas praised.

The old man and the young boy made their way down the hallway, a very long hallway, it seemed to Joey. He didn't know why it hadn't occurred to him before. He guessed it must have been because he had always been in such a hurry. But now, it reminded him of the time he'd gotten lost at his grandfather's ranch. A wisp of fear ran up Joey's back, like a soft breeze blowing through the trees outside his bedroom window on a dark, stormy night. He reached up and grabbed Nicholas's hand, then squeezed it. A gentle squeeze in return somehow made him feel a whole lot better. When they walked into the den, Caesar was already waiting. He greeted them with a loud "woof" and then dropped into place next to the big cushioned chair.

"Did you have a good nap, Nicholas?" Joey asked.

"It was a fine nap, nice and long, just the way I like it."

"That's good. I left you a note. I said I would come back later, and so, here I am."

"Indeed you are. Do your mother and father know where you are?"

"Yeah. They said I could come as long as I was home before dark. So I gotta go … when does it start getting dark anyways?"

"I'd say about four-thirty or—"

"Before then," Joey interrupted.

"We'll be sure that you're on your way before then. Do you hear that Caesar? Don't delay the boy. How are things at home, Joey? Any word on your father's mill?" the old man queried.

"Oh, I meant to tell ya. My Uncle Frank got into a really bad accident today. He's not really my uncle, he's my dad's best friend, but I call him Uncle Frank 'cause I knew him since I was born. Anyways, one of the thingies that holds stuff in place broke, and a big beam came down and hit Uncle Frank in the head, and now he's unconscientious. I'm not sure what that means, but it must be bad. Dad says there's no way that they can keep the mill open now, 'cause it's too dangerous."

"I think you mean unconscious."

"Yeah, that."

"Well, that means he's in a coma. It's like being asleep, but you can't wake up," Nick explained. "And you're right, that is bad. I do hope Uncle Frank will be all right. It would be a shame if all those people lost their jobs because someone was injured. It doesn't seem quite fair."

"That's what I said to my dad—" Joey began. But he was interrupted in mid-sentence by Nicholas, who was taken by one of his coughing spells. The fit lasted for quite a while before subsiding. When it was over, Joey felt a chill, one that seemed to fill the whole room. Caesar felt it too. Joey could tell, because his ears were pointed straight up, like the hairs on the back of Joey's neck when Grandpa told ghost stories.

"Nicholas, are you all right?"

"I'm fine," Nicholas assured, all the while hiding the handkerchief with its ever-increasing red stains. Joey wasn't quite convinced but didn't particularly want to know anymore. He'd had plenty of bad news to dwell upon today. But still, there was a part of him that was more than a little worried.

"I just need to sit down for a while. Old people get tired much quicker than you youngsters do," Nicholas explained.

"I guess that's true, 'cause I'm not tired at all," came Joey's youthful reply.

"It's a good thing too. Caesar needs another walk, and I don't have the strength to do it. Would you mind?"

"By myself? Do you think I can?"

"Why, sure you can. You're a strong young man. Caesar will take it easy on you. Won't you, boy? Now run along, the leash is hanging next to the front door. And remember," Nicholas paused for a moment, then came the unison response, "wherever Caesar wishes to go."

By then, Joey was already half way into the hall and Caesar was another twenty feet ahead of that. The front door slamming was Nicholas's cue. He picked up the phone.

"Hello? Erik? I'm ready to finish that little project we've been working on. I'll explain what I want. You bring it over in the morning for me to sign. No arguments."

Meanwhile, outside Caesar was having more fun than he'd had in years. It felt good to be able to run and frolic in the snow without the worry of Nicholas keeping up. It was comforting to have a new friend that was as anxious to play as he was, someone who didn't mind a little rough-housing. He was glad Joey had come along when he did. He'd noticed a big change in Nicholas as well. He smiled more. He had a sense of purpose again. It was a peace of mind that Caesar had been trying to provide since his arrival, shortly after Gladdys had passed away. He'd felt it was his responsibility. That's why he'd been brought to Nicholas in the first place. He had made great progress in healing the old man's pain. It takes a lot of time to recover after someone you love, and have shared so much of life with, is no longer there. But, for all of the friendship, loyalty, and love that he had given, this young boy with his indomitable spirit had been able to do what he had not. For this, Caesar would be forever grateful, not to mention somewhat smitten.

"Whoa, Caesar. Not so fast, I have short legs. I can't run as fast as you. Besides, this snow is too deep." In that very breath, Joey collapsed into a snow bank. "See? I told you I couldn't keep up with you." In seconds Caesar was there, licking his face, tickling his ear with the hairs around his mouth, and leaving a large wet spot on the tip of his chin. Joey reached out and grabbed the faithful companion around the neck and squeezed as hard as he could. "I love you, Caesar!" The feeling was mutual.

"I'm tired. Let's go back in the house now," Joey panted.

"Good day, Erik, and thank you," Nicholas said as he hung up the phone.

With that done, the old man leaned back in his chair and closed his eyes. He had just nodded off when Joey and Caesar scrambled through the front door. It was like something out of an episode of *The Keystone Cops.* Caesar entered first. His wet paws hit the freshly waxed hardwood floor, and he went sliding into the far wall like a snow sled hitting an ice patch coming down Davis Hill. Joey stumbled in after him, leash in hand, with a dazed look on his face. Caesar shook his head back and forth wildly trying to regain his senses. He very carefully made his way to his feet only to have them slip out from under him once again. In direct response, Joey made an almost parallel reaction, falling to the floor in convulsive laughter. They were quite a pair. Once both of them were upright and under control, they made their way down the long hallway to the den. As Joey entered the room, he saw Nicholas lying motionless in the chair. His heart and jaw dropped simultaneously.

"Nicholas! Nicholas! Wake up!" he screamed.

"What's all the fuss? What are we hollering about?" Nick mumbled as he returned to a sitting position.

"I thought you were dead." Joey began to cry.

"Not yet. Give me a chance to put my affairs in order first." Nicholas chuckled. "Now shut off the faucet. I am perfectly fine." Nicholas glanced at the clock on the wall. "It's almost four-thirty. Shouldn't you be heading home?"

"Oh, yeah. I promised Mom. I gotta go. Bye, Nicholas. Bye, Caesar." Like a flash he was gone. Caesar watched as the boy flew out the door. He walked over, licked his master's hand, and lay down at his feet. Nicholas coughed.

Contrary to the walk to Nicholas's house, the walk home seemed like it took forever. Everything that had happened today was running through Joey's brain, like one of Uncle Dave's (his real uncle) home movies, the ones he made everyone watch each time the family got together at his house for special occasions. Joey's imagination became a movie projector playing the events of the day on the back of his mind like it was a silver screen. Breakfast. Taking out the garbage. Caesar's first walk. It kept going. How good the hot chocolate had tasted. The pride he felt after polishing the gold coin. Then coming home to find out about Uncle Frank's accident and how the mill would have to close down. He remembered what Dad had said about Christmas not being about money. The walk back to Nicholas's. Sneaking Caesar his bread crusts. The long walk down the giant hallway. Nicholas's coughing fit. The picture of Caesar crashing into the wall. Finding Nicholas asleep in his chair and thinking he was dead. It had been a long day already, and it wasn't over yet.

Joey walked through the front door to find his mom in the kitchen washing dishes and his dad on the phone with the hospital. There had been no change in Uncle Frank's condition. Joey went upstairs to his room and changed his clothes.

He was confused about what to do next. He lay down on his bed, and just as he fell asleep, a solitary tear rolled down the creases of his face onto his pillow.

Joey awoke to the smell of freshly cooked sweet potatoes covered with brown sugar and vanilla. The aroma was wafting up the stairwell and into his room, and it put a smile back on his face. Even though it might only be temporary, it sure felt good to turn that frown upside down. Joey leapt from his bed and raced down the stairs. It felt as though his feet weren't even touching the steps as he flew down that staircase. It's amazing how hungry you can get, just by taking a nap. When he reached the bottom of the stairs, Joey could smell the rest of dinner: honey ham and mashed potatoes and gravy. He strolled into the kitchen and started to sit down in his chair when Dad spoke up.

"Did you wash those filthy mitts, young man?"

"Oh! Sorry. Nope. I didn't, but I will right now." He raced back up the stairs.

"This meal looks scrumptious, dear. How are you ever going to top this for Christmas?"

"Oh, I have a few tricks up my sleeve, and thank you, darling." She kissed him tenderly and pulled back to look into his eyes. "I love you! Don't worry, dear, things will work out. You'll see. God has a way of taking care of things. Sometimes we don't have any way of understanding it, but it works out. This is no different."

"Thank you, sweetie. I know you're right, because he brought me you, and that little boy upstairs. By the way, I love you, too." With that, he returned the favor with a long, heartfelt kiss, one that made them both blush just a little bit.

At that moment, Joey entered. "Oooooo, Mommy and Daddy sitting in a tree. K-I-S-S-I-N-G." Joey laughed and sat back down at the table.

Mom and Dad laughed as well. Joey took in the vast menu of dinner choices that were laid out on the dining room table. Everything was there, even the vegetables. Tonight it was green beans. Actually green beans weren't so bad. Conversation was typical: Nicholas, Uncle Frank, the mill, Christmas, and the weather, among other things. Dinner ended with the fidgety little boy pushing his chair away from the table.

"Dad, may I be excused, please?" Joey asked. "I need to find something to make Nicholas for Christmas."

"Sure, son. What did you have in mind?"

"I don't know yet. Do you think you could help me, Dad?"

"I don't see why not. You figure out what you want to make, and I'll do what I can to lend a hand."

"Where do I start?" Joey was puzzled.

"Why don't you try in the woodshed?"

"Oh, yeah! That's the perfect place. Thank you, Daddy." With that, Joey rushed out the back door toward the woodshed.

"Well, that was easy enough." Dad chuckled as the door slammed shut.

Outside Joey was just opening the door to the shed when it occurred to him how beneficial it would have been to grab his coat on the way out. No matter. He was here now, and he had to find something he could use to make Nicholas a Christmas present. Upon entering the shack, Joey gazed in amazement at the display of tools and knick-knacks that hung from the walls. There were saws and chisels and hammers and tons of other oddly shaped items that Joey, in his wildest imagination, couldn't begin to figure out how to use. Then he looked over to the woodpile. Yep, that was where he would find his desire.

He zigzagged his way through and climbed over the various half-finished projects that Father had started over the years and never quite had time to finish. He tripped and fell when trying to high step the bottom half of the old china cabinet that he'd knocked over and broken when he was only four. Dad had brought it out here to put it back together, and after a week of frustration decided that Mom deserved a new one instead. He could have fixed it, he'd said. It was just that it wouldn't be worth all that effort when Mom's birthday was coming up and he had seen one at the carpentry shop that would be perfect for that bare corner in the dining room. Continuing his trek Joey had to laugh at the whole chain of events. He really had almost bitten it big time. He had just managed to catch himself as his tummy hit the cold floor. He stood up and clapped his hands together to get all the dust off, which in turn made him sneeze and stumble right back into the same cabinet he had just climbed over. He nearly fell again. But now, with that obstacle out of the way, he had a clear path to the woodpile. He marched over, dedicated to the task at hand, knowing that what he was looking for was right there in front of him. He fumbled through a few odd-shaped pieces. One of them had grain lines that reminded him of the varicose veins on grandma Schafer's ankles. Sorting and sorting until, at last he found it. It was perfect. He didn't know exactly what it was perfect for, but he knew it was perfect. After making his way back through the maze of impediments, he strode out the door of that little building with a look on his face that must have rivaled that of Columbus after discovering the New World.

"I found it! I found it!" Joey shouted as he crashed through the back door and into the kitchen.

"What? What?" his mother hollered back as she put the last of the dinner dishes in the cupboard.

"Nicholas's present!" he exclaimed.

"Well, that's wonderful, dear. What is it?"

"I ... I ... I don't really know exactly."

"Whatever it is, sweetie, it ... it looks... perfect," Mother stammered.

"I know. Isn't it great?" Off he went, up to his room.

It is strange how life can change in a heartbeat. One moment you can feel like the world is about to run you down with a snowplow and then suddenly something happens. Your focus changes and you feel a new spirit within you. It happens a whole lot easier when you're seven than it does when you're eighty-nine. But it happens just the same.

Nicholas awoke to the warmth of Caesar's tongue as it lapped across his forearm.

"Thank you, my friend," he said as he stretched and made his way to his feet. "I needed to wake up and take care of some things before it got to be too late." He then crossed to the telephone and rang Erik's number. "Hello, Erik? How's it coming? Yes. Good. Very well then, a few more minor details and I think we can wrap this up."

Joey had been pondering now for more than half an hour, trying to decide what exactly it was that his scrap of wood was perfect for. And still he didn't have a clue as to what it might become. He was sure he was just about to come up with a great idea when the door to his room opened. It was his mother and father coming to tuck him in.

"Okay, young man, it's time for bed."

"Aww, Dad. Do I have to? I still haven't figured out what to make Nicholas."

"Yes, son, you do. It will come to you. Why don't you try writing it down on a piece of paper?"

"That's a neat idea," Joey said as he rummaged to find a piece of paper and a pencil.

"Tomorrow, though. Tonight you have to go to bed." Joey, after a little more argumentation, was finally persuaded to put his pajamas on while his dad found a story to read to him out of the Bible.

"Here's a good one," Dad said as he sat down in the chair next to the bed, while Joey's mother tucked her little man in. Dad proceeded to read the story of how Jesus was known as the carpenter's son, and how no one could really believe that he would ever be anything special just because his dad built stuff. And that was all Joey heard. Before Father could get any further, Joey was asleep. It had indeed been a long and trying day. Sleep came very easily, and well deserved, to the little boy with the red hair and freckles.

After Mom and Dad left, Joey woke just long enough to say his prayers.

"Dear Jesus, things sure can get messed up, can't they? I wonder if your life was this scary when you were a little boy. I think it probably was. Anyways, I pray for Mommy and Daddy and Grandma and Grandpa and all my friends and their families. Mostly I pray for Uncle Frank. I pray that you will make him all better, and I also pray that you will take care of Nicholas, 'cause I think that there's something wrong with him, too. Thank you for being born, so we can celebrate Christmas. I love you. AMEN."

Day 4:

Tuesday, December 24 (Christmas Eve)

It was days like today that made Joey glad he was just seven years old. He, however, didn't know that is was days like today that made him glad. But he was, just the same. It was things like the icicles that hung from the gutter outside his window. They would form at night and be hanging there in the morning. The sun would shine on them and Joey could see the different colors as the rays of light bounced off. It was like looking into a kaleidoscope. As the clouds would pass, the colors would change and shift. Then as the day wore on and it got warmer, the ice would begin to melt and drip, drip, drip to the ground, making hole patterns in the snow.

(One morning Joey could have sworn that it actually spelled out his name.) In the afternoon, those solidified cones of ice would detach and bang to the ground in intermittent succession. It was like God was playing a sonata and each of the icicles was a hammer pounding the ground like strings on nature's piano.

Joey was just getting his shirt pulled over his head when he saw Bobby and Michael coming down the street toward his house. He had barely finished with his shirt and put his socks and shoes on when the doorbell rang. Joey charged down the stairs and reached for the door. Upon opening it, he saw his two pals standing there. Each had a puzzled look on his face.

"Hey! How did you get away?" Michael asked.

"Yeah. We thought you were dead," added Bobby

Though he didn't do it very often, Joey saw the chance to gloat a little. And seeing as how they had left him there to die, he felt it only appropriate to take advantage of this opportunity.

"I told you he was nice. He gave me hot chocolate and let me polish his old coin and he let me take Caesar for a walk all by myself. So now I'm going to make him a Christmas present, and my dad's going to help me." Joey took a deep breath, let out a heavy sigh, and finished. "I can't come out and play right now, so you're going to have come back later."

"But ... but ... but ... ," Bobby stuttered.

"We just wanted to ... ," Michael started. Just then Joey's mom called.

"Joey! Come and eat breakfast."

"Coming!" Joey hollered back. "I gotta go you guys. Come back after lunch time. 'K?" Joey nodded a casual good-bye and closed the door.

When he entered the kitchen, he sensed a more relaxed feeling in the house. It reminded him of a time when he was playing with Dad's razor and pretending to shave (even though Dad had told him a bunch of times not to). He heard his dad yell his name and thought he was going to get caught. It scared the stuffing out of him until he realized that Dad just wanted him to take out the garbage. That was the kind of relaxed feeling that permeated the room.

"Here you go, dear," Mother said as she set his bowl on the table. "You should have some toast and orange juice in just one moment, honey."

"Thank you, Mom," Joey replied. Breakfast this morning was boiled rice with milk and brown sugar. It was even better than oatmeal. Well, maybe not better, but as good, and it was different.

"Well, Joe, I have some good news."

Joey knew it.

"It looks like Uncle Frank is going to be all right."

At this point Joey's dad walked over, put a hand on each of Joey's shoulders, bent down, looked into his eyes, smiled, and then kissed him on the forehead.

"What was that for?" Joey asked.

"That's for being faithful in believing that Uncle Frank would get better."

"I knew God would take care of him," Joey stated confidently.

"Now, with the mill down for the holidays and the pending closure, I just hope he can find a way to pay those medical bills," Father added.

"I'm just grateful it wasn't any worse than it was," came Mother's look-on-the-bright-side response.

"Agreed," Father said.

"Oh, Joey, who was that at the door just before breakfast?" Mom asked.

"It was Bobby and Michael."

"Well, what did they want?"

"I don't know."

"You don't know? What do you mean, you don't know?"

"I never asked 'em."

"Oh. Well. All right then," Mother said.

After he was done with breakfast, Joey fiddled with his spoon until he couldn't hold it in any longer.

"Mom and Dad, may I be excused from the table so I can work on Nicholas's present?"

"Why certainly, son. Put your dishes in the sink first," Father requested.

"Okay. I will."

"Any idea what it might be yet, Joe?"

"Not yet. I'm still kinda workin' on it."

"Let me know if you need any help."

"You got it, Dad." In a flash he was on his way up the stairs to get to work.

Back at the Brandon mansion, Nicholas was just finishing his signature on some important-looking documents.

"That should do it then, right Erik?"

"Yes, sir. That is all of the changes that you requested. But are you sure this is what you want to do? I mean, this is everything you have. Are you sure that you want to put it into something that you have no real knowledge of?"

"Erik, do I appear to be delusional or not in my right mind to you?

"Well … er … no, sir! You seem to be perfectly capable to me."

"Then why do you question my judgment on this matter?"

"It is not a matter of question, sir. It's just that … well … I only want to be sure this is what you want."

"If it wasn't what I wanted, then it would have been very ridiculous of me to waste your time and my money to have you put it all together. Isn't that true?"

"Yes, sir. I suppose it would."

"Good. Now if you might be so kind as to make this all legal and binding, I believe we are through."

"Very well then, sir. Good day."

"Good day, Erik, and thank you."

"You're welcome, sir." At that, Erik put the papers into his briefcase and walked out the front door.

Friends are
a blessing
from God.

That was it. After what seemed like hours of thinking and experimenting, after countless efforts to make something and to say just the right thing, this was all that his seven-year-old brain could come up with.

"Good grief!" Joey exclaimed. "How can I give this to Nicholas? It isn't even a present. It's just a bunch of words. And I still have to make something out of that piece of wood I found. Shoot! I'm never going to be able to make Nicholas a present in time for Christmas. He'll think that I don't love him. I just gotta make something."

Just then, Joey's bedroom door opened. It was Father.

"So Joe, how are we doing on that Christmas gift?"

"Oh, Dad. I can't think of anything. I'm terrible at making presents. Nicholas will think.... oh, just forget it." Joey couldn't go on. He was on the verge of tears when his dad spoke up.

"Hold on there, young man. What do you mean you can't think of anything? Show me what you have so far."

"That's what I mean. I don't have nothing. All I got is this silly piece of paper.

"Let me see it." Father reached out his hand, and Joey put a small piece of paper into it. The compassionate patriarch peered down at the pleated piece of parchment, and as he read, an ever-increasing grin of appreciation crept across his face. First, there was that glimmer of pride in the eyes, then the wrinkle at the base of each nostril that led to a twitch at both corners of his mouth until it was a full fledged beam of adoration and esteem.

"It seems to me, son, that you've done a wonderful job of making a present here."

"What are you talking about, Dad? It's just a piece of paper with a bunch of words on it."

"No, Joe. If you look again, I think you'll see something different." Joey grabbed the paper from his father's hand and read it again.

"What do you mean? It's the same thing that it was before."

"You're not looking at it in the right way, Joe. What I see is a beautiful sentiment, worthy of some sort of permanence."

"What are you talking about?" Joey was baffled.

"Where is that piece of wood you pulled out of the shed?"

"Over on my dresser. But I haven't made it into anything yet."

"Hold your horses, son. I'm getting to that. Now if we take this simple slab of lumber and this silly piece of paper as you call it and put them together as one, what we have is a great Christmas gift."

"I still don't get it, Dad," Joey replied, frustrated by the whole thing.

"Will you trust me, son? You have a wonderful present here. All it needs is a little finalizing."

"Okay, Dad. Whatever you say, I guess. I trust you," Joey said, still not convinced that he had done much of anything.

"You'll see in due time. You did a great job, son. I'm very proud of you. Now clean up this mess, while I put a little work in on this." Joey watched his father exit and wondered what it was that he had done that made his dad so proud of him. Then he looked around his room, only to find that someone had made a terrible mess of it. There were wads of paper everywhere. As he cleaned, he was reminded of two years ago when a huge hailstorm had littered the front yard with hailstones the size of walnuts. What a racket that had made. He remembered thinking that the house was going to fall down, so he had run into his parents' room and slept in their bed with them. What a baby he had been. Joey's reminiscing was interrupted by the doorbell. He finished picking up the last of the paper hailstones and headed for the door. Again it was Bobby and Michael. They had come to play.

"Hello!" Joey, Bobby, and Michael all said at the same time. This was quickly followed by a huge belly laugh then a short period of silence and ended with Mother walking out of the kitchen.

"Joey! Time for lunch. Oh! Hello boys. How are you?"

"We're great, Mrs. Adams!" Bobby took the role of spokesperson.

"Well, have you eaten lunch yet, boys?

"Nope. We haven't." Michael took his turn.

"How would you like to eat with us?"

"What are you having?" Bobby and Michael asked.

"That isn't an answer, boys. That is a question, but to answer your question, beef stew and cornbread with butter and honey."

"Oh, boy!" Joey chimed in. "Can we have some of your strawberry jam too, Mom?"

"Please!" they all shouted together.

"Sure you can." The boys headed for the kitchen. "Hold on a minute. Bobby and Michael, is this going to be okay with your mother?"

"Yeah. She won't care. We were just going to have sandwiches, but we said we didn't want none, so she told us to go out and play," Bobby explained.

"All right then. You gentlemen go and get washed up, and then we'll eat." The three starving youths trotted upstairs. It's funny how at the time of Bobby and Michael's arrival food hadn't really even crossed their minds. But now, after the mention of cornbread and Mom's homemade strawberry jam, they felt as if they might just die of starvation before they reached the bathroom.

Meanwhile in the kitchen, Mother was pulling a pan of cornbread out of the oven. The smell of fresh baked cornbread has to be one of the all time best aromas to ever waft from a kitchen. The stew was already dished and waiting on the table as Mom sliced the cornbread into nice big squares. The three boys were taking their seats as Mom put the whipped butter, honey, and jam on the table. Each was grabbing his spoon with one hand and reaching for a piece of cornbread with the other when Mom's voice stopped them.

"Aren't we forgetting something, gentlemen?"

"What?" came the boys' unison reply.

"Shouldn't we thank the one responsible for this meal?" Mother teased.

"Oh! Thank you, Mom," Joey spoke up.

"Not me, you goofball. I was referring to God. How about saying a little grace?"

"Oops!" The boys laughed out loud. Then they folded their hands and expressed their gratitude, each in his own words, to the provider. Bobby and Michael each had two huge helpings of stew and two of the largest pieces of cornbread they could find. Joey ate a very generous portion of stew himself, along with a couple of the smaller sections of cornbread. The boys ate until they couldn't eat anymore.

"Mom, could we be excused please?" Joey asked.

"Wash and dry your bowls and put them away. Then you can go," Mother stated firmly.

"Thank you, Mrs. Adams. That was a great lunch," gushed Bobby and Michael.

"You are very welcome, boys. Thank you for cleaning up after yourselves." After finishing the dishes, the boys made their way out to the wood-shed. Father was just finishing up his project as the door opened.

"Good afternoon, boys. How was lunch?"

"It was wonderful," answered Joey.

"Yeah. We ate so much I think we won't hafta eat for a week," Michael reported.

"Your wife sure is a good cook, Mr. Adams," Bobby said as he rubbed his belly for emphasis.

"She sure is. Probably the best cook in all of Vermont, and you be sure and tell her I said so, will ya?" Father laughed as he winked at the three attentive youngsters. "So what do you gents have planned for this afternoon?"

"What time is it anyway?" Bobby asked.

"Going on 2:30," Father replied.

"Dang! We have to go and finish our chores before our dad gets back from town," Bobby explained regretfully.

"Bye, Joey. Bye, Mr. Adams." With that, the two older boys hurried off.

Joey watched as his dad began cleaning up the wood scraps and carefully brushing out all of his tools. He was always so particular about his tools and making sure the area where he worked was neat and tidy. He was very deliberate and precise about where everything went. It was like watching a beaver building a dam or a bird building a nest. Joey figured it must be a grown-up thing.

"Dad, how come you never just leave your stuff there when you're just going to use it again, anyways?"

"Well, son, you know how you couldn't find your shoes the other day when we were ready to go to town?"

"Yeah," Joey replied sheepishly.

"That's why."

"Huh? You put your tools away because ... "
Joey paused a moment to try and let it sink in. "I
couldn't find my shoes?"

"Yes. Well, not exactly. I put my tools away
because I want to know where they are when I
need them. If I just left them wherever I was
when I was done using them, the next time I had
to fix something or make something, I might not
remember where they were. Then I would have
to hunt for them, like you did your shoes, and I
might not get to do what I intended to do. Do
you understand?"

"Sorta, I do," Joey said.

"It all comes down to pride and respect, Joe. I
worked very hard to be able to afford to buy nice
tools and have a workshop. I want to be able to
keep these things for a long time and work in a
place where I feel safe. Are you getting it yet?"

"You mean like at the mill. If everybody
took good care of the equipment and made sure
everything was put away and worked good, then
Uncle Frank might not have gotten hurt and
the mill wouldn't have to close," Joey explained,
excited by the fact that he was finally beginning
to grasp this whole concept.

"Very good, Joe," Father lauded. "That's pretty much the idea. If we take care of our things, then they will take care of us."

"So what were you doin' anyways, Dad?"

"I was just finishing up a little handy work on Nicholas's Christmas present."

"What Christmas present?"

"The one you made for him."

"Oh! That Christmas present. What is it?" Joey remembered what Dad had said about a perfect gift for Nicholas. He remembered that he was supposed to trust his dad about the fact that he had done something wonderful. Now, he just wanted to know what it was.

"Hold on." Father chuckled as he walked over to the workbench. When he got there, Joey saw him pick something up, but he couldn't make out exactly what it was. Dad seemed to be intentionally hiding it from him, but maybe that was just his curiosity getting the better of him. He saw Dad take a deep breath and then caught a glimpse of sawdust in the air.

"Okay, Joe. Come on over here." Joey rushed to the bench, his mind in a quandary. What could it be? When he arrived, Father had the present lying out on the workbench.

After what seemed like an hour of just looking at it, Joey spoke. In a voice that trembled in awe, yet flowed with pride, he said, "It *is* perfect. I knew my present would be perfect, and it is. Oh, Daddy, Daddy, I can't believe it. Did I really think of this?"

"Sure you did, son. You picked out the wood. You came up with the words. I just put them together for you." The end result was beyond anything Joey might have imagined.

Resting there in front of him was that ideal piece of wood he'd been so lucky to find and etched upon it in beautiful block lettering were the six words he had spent hours coming up with: *FRIENDS ARE A BLESSING FROM GOD.* It would be perfect for Nick's mantle, right next to the shiny gold coin.

"Yeah. A nice coat of stain, some shellac, and it should be done by morning," Father stated confidently and with the slightest hint of a job well done.

Inside the house, Mother was getting things ready for Christmas dinner. She was cutting up vegetables and grinding herbs, chopping up the dried bread into little squares, and mixing the whole concoction in a huge bowl. Joey and his father walked into the kitchen just as she was scraping what was left of the cornbread into the mixing bowl.

"There. That ought to be the perfect touch for your Christmas stuffing, boys," she announced. "Darling, will you bring me that pie tin, and Joey you can put this bowl in the refrigerator."

"Sure, Mom." Joey promptly stashed the large bowl in the already overly crowded refrigerator. "Hey, Mom, how come you're making all this stuff now, when Christmas isn't until tomorrow?" Joey asked.

"There are a lot of things to do, dear, far more than we could possibly get done on Christmas morning."

"What time are we going to eat?" queried the curious youth

"Around one or two o'clock, the same time we eat every Christmas."

"Are we going to have a lot of people at our house?" An idea was slowly forming in Joey's head.

"Let me see." Mother pondered the question a moment. "No, not really. No more than usual. Frank won't be here, what with him still being in the hospital and all. But still, there are a lot of things that have to be done."

"Then do you think Nicholas could come to our house for Christmas? I bet he hasn't had a Christmas dinner in a long time." The thought fully conceived, Joey sprung it on his parents like a cat attacking a ball of yarn. It was sneaky, yet full of enthusiasm, and with great potential to create quite a mess. Nonetheless, it was done.

"Well … uh … Joe … " Dad stammered.

"We do have a little extra room, but … " Mom tried to rescue.

"Oh, what the heck." Dad relented. "Any friend of Joey's is a friend of mine," he mocked playfully. "What do you say, honey? Shall we set another place for dinner?"

"Sure. Why not? The more the merrier, right? After all, it is Christmas, and no one should have to be alone for the holidays."

"Yippee!" shouted Joey, then he started jumping up and down and hollering. "Thank you! Thank you! Thank you!" Now that he had started bouncing, he couldn't seem to stop. "Can I go over there right now and ask Nicholas if he wants to come? Can I? Can I? Can I?

"Yes, you may," Mother consented.

"But grab your coat first, kangaroo boy," Father added.

"I will," Joey replied as he hopped over to his coat, picked it up, and then bounded out the door, all the while his parents wondering how such a little boy could have such a big heart.

"We have a lot of work to do," Father said.

"We certainly do," Mother agreed.

It was a beautiful day. The sun was out and the spattered clouds were floating across the sky like the marshmallows in one of Nicholas's tasty cups of hot cocoa. The soft breeze was really quite warm for this time of year. So warm, in fact, that Joey didn't even have to put his coat on during his walk to the big house on the hill. *Nicholas is sure going to be surprised,* Joey thought to himself as he scurried up the winding drive to the front of the house. It was funny, but somehow that big brass knocker seemed a little closer today than it had yesterday. Still, it was far out of Joey's reach, so he rang the bell and waited. Caesar had been whining impatiently at the door for quite a while before Nicholas finally arrived to open it.

"Hello, Joey," came Nick's cheerful greeting. Caesar greeted him, too, with a big wet slop of dog tongue across his cheek. "Come on in, young man. How are we today?"

"I'm fine, Nicholas," Joey declared. "It sure is a beautiful day outside."

"It most definitely is. And what brings you to our side of town so late in the afternoon?"

"I came to tell ya something, actually two things. I don't know which one to say first, 'cause they're both really neat. Actually I have three things."

"Hold on there, little one. Slow down. I can only listen so fast. You may not be able to run as fast as your friends, but I'll bet you talk quicker than any of them."

"Yeah, I think I prolly do, exspecially when I get excited."

"Now, take your time and start with the last thing you thought of first," Nicholas advised.

"Okay. Let's see. Oh yeah, my Uncle Frank is gonna be all right. He's only got a severe … ," Joey paused a moment to get the word, "concussion. Is that right?"

"Yes, Joey, it is. That is very good," Nicholas praised. "And good news, too."

"But he's still in the hospital, so he won't be able to come to our house for Christmas dinner."

"I'm sorry to hear that," the old man sympathized.

"So I asked my mom and dad if you could have Christmas dinner with us instead, and they said yes. So … can you?"

"Well! That is quite an offer. I haven't been anywhere for Christmas dinner in at least five years. It would be rude of me to decline such heartfelt generosity."

"Does that mean yes?" Joey cut in.

"I suppose it does," Nick concluded.

"Oh, goody!" Joey started hopping again.

"Okay. Okay. Stop with the up and down stuff. I'm starting to get motion sickness. Now suppose you tell me the third piece of news."

"Oh yeah, I almost forgot. I made you something for Christmas. I made it all by myself. Well, my dad helped me some. But it was my idea, and I picked it out. I had to make you something 'cause I don't have any money.

"Presents that you make yourself are the very best kind of presents. I used to make all of Gladdys's presents myself. And she would make mine. On Christmas morning we'd make hot chocolate then sit by the tree and exchange them. Gladdys used to love sitting by the fire, drinking hot cocoa, and reading a book. I recall one year when I made her a special bookmark. I designed it with a long straight edge on the top for keeping her place on the page. Then there was a space about the size of a line of type, and then another straight edge for the next line. In the space between straight edges I wrote: 'I love you. I love you. I love you.' I called it her 'reading between the lines' bookmark. I believe she cried over that one. Some of my fondest memories are of those cold winter mornings by this very fireplace," Nicholas reminisced. "But I'm digressing ... "

"What does that mean?" Joey interrupted.

"It just means I was talking about something other than what we were talking about," Nicholas explained.

"Oh! What were we talking about? I digressed, too." Joey laughed.

"We were talking about presents and dinner." The old man chuckled. "By the way, when is this gala event scheduled to begin?"

"Mom said we would be eating about one or two o'clock, but I'll come over earlier than that to give you your present. Then we can walk to my house." As Joey spoke he could see Nicholas's eyes close. He noticed the way his chest heaved as he breathed, and he realized that he had been coughing more and more all the time. "Nicholas, are you feeling okay? You don't look so good." That nagging feeling was back, and it was getting worse by the second.

"I'll be fine," he replied convincingly. "I just took Caesar for his walk, and I'm getting too old to keep up with him. Joey, do you think you could take care of Caesar for me? I mean, take him for walks, give him baths, make sure he has lots of food, and most of all, plenty of love. Do you suppose you could handle all of those chores?"

"Sure, I could. I already took him for a walk, and that's the hardest part," Joey replied undaunted.

"That's great. I think you can, too. And Caesar will make it easy on you, 'cause he likes you. I'm just too tired anymore. I need my rest."

"You want me to see if I can stay the night and take care of you?" Joey offered.

"No. No. You go on home. It's starting to get late, and you don't want to break that promise to your mother. I will be all right. You run along and I'll see you in the morning. I can't wait to see the present you made for me. I'll bet it's very nice." Nicholas started to cough but stopped it in time for Joey not to notice.

"Well, okay. You sure you don't need me for nuthin'?"

"I'm sure. You run along. Caesar will walk you to the door." On demand, the compliant canine got up, trotted over to the little boy, and led him to the front door.

It was much later than Joey had realized. He would have to hurry to get home before dark. There was something about that bothersome apprehension that urged his legs to move just a little faster, not only how late it was, but the realization that Nick was sick. He made the trip home in record time and entered the backyard just as the first star flickered into view. Joey took a moment to look up at it and make a wish. "Star light, star bright, first star I see tonight, wish I may, wish you might grant this wish I wish tonight." No one could ever know what he wished for, or else it wouldn't come true.

Mom and Dad were still bustling around the kitchen preparing for the events of the next day when Joey entered through the back door.

"Whew! I made it," he proudly proclaimed.

"You sure did, little man, and just in the *nick* of time," Father said with a wry smirk on his face. "Joe, why don't you head upstairs and wash up while your mom and I finish, then I have something to show you."

"Okay, Dad, but what is it?" Joey inched in a little closer.

"The bathroom is that way," Dad said as he spun Joey around and directed him toward the stairs. "You'll find out when you get back down here. As a matter of fact, why don't you just get in the bath and soak for a while? We have quite a bit left to do, and that will give us a little more time."

"Oh, Dad, do I have to?" Joey whined. But he could tell by the look on his father's face that arguing would do him no good, so he trotted upstairs to the bathroom.

He wasn't exactly sure what it was about taking a bath that he didn't like. He wasn't even sure he didn't like taking a bath. But every time Mom or Dad told him to do it, he felt repelled. It was like the words "Joey, take a bath" set off some force field mechanism in his brain that wouldn't allow him to enjoy the thought of soaking in a tub of hot water. There were times, when he thought of it on his own, that it sounded like a really good idea. But for some reason when his parents told him to, it was the last thing on earth he wanted to do. He had to convince himself that it wasn't really a bath; it was some sort of underwater expedition. Well, now the adventure was on. He turned the faucet handle marked "H" three quarter turns to the right, then the one with a "C" on it, one half turn in the same direction. Dad had said to only let the tub fill with about four to six inches of water, so he had to be sure and watch it carefully. In the meantime, the tiny scuba diver extracted himself from his clothes and wrote his name in the condensation that had formed on the medicine cabinet mirror.

Downstairs, Mother and Father were hard at it, putting together elements of the following day's feast. Mom was setting out the dough for the homemade rolls so it could rise. Pop was peeling potatoes to be mashed for one of his favorite side dishes.

"Looks like we're going to have a late supper tonight, dear," Father commented.

"I guess so," Mother responded. "Something simple appears to be in order; something that won't add too drastically to our mess."

"How about grilled cheese sandwiches and tomato soup?" he suggested.

"That's a fine idea, dear. You grab the bread, cheese, and butter, and I'll get the soup pan and skillet." Once their scavenger hunt was complete, they worked in unison to put the alternative evening meal together.

"If you don't need me for anything else, I think I'll go and check on our little drowning rat."

"I can handle it from here. You go ahead." With permission granted, Father made his way upstairs to the bathroom door. Listening very closely, he could hear the sound of a motor boat trolling the waters on the other side. Satisfied that all was well, he went to the linen closet and grabbed a towel. On his way back he found a pair of Joey's pajamas, along with his bathrobe and slippers. When Dad entered, Joey was standing in the tub dripping, looking every bit the drowned rat Father had gone in search of.

"Here. Dry off and put these on, then pick up your dirty clothes and put them in the hamper. When you're done, come downstairs and eat," Father stated while unloading his arms onto the top of the wicker clothes hamper.

"What about what you were going to show me?" Joey prompted.

"After we finish our food. You have an amazing memory for someone who forgets to close the front door half of the time. Now hurry up," Father urged as he closed the door behind him and headed back downstairs.

Joey grabbed the towel and wrapped it around his body nice and tight, like a silkworm in his cocoon. He always waited for the tub to drain completely before he got out so he could watch the last of the water spiral down the drain and make that gurgley sound. That done, he climbed out of the claw-footed, cast iron basin and stepped onto the cold ceramic tile floor. First, he rubbed his hair with the towel, then he shook his head in a manner very similar to the method used by Caesar shortly after smashing into the wall at Nick's house. He dried his hair again and quickly followed with his shoulders, his torso, and finally his arms and legs. He slipped into his pajamas, the flannel ones with pictures of cowboys and Indians on them. Next, he slid his feet into his slippers and an arm into each sleeve of his bathrobe. Now fully dressed, he proceeded to pick up the clothes he'd taken off and throw them into the hamper like he was playing basketball at the YMCA. Then he dried the floor with his towel and tossed that in with the rest of the dirty laundry. Now it was time to eat. He hurried down the stairs and into the kitchen. He could smell and hear the buttered bread browning in the skillet as he entered the room. Dad was already seated at the table with a large bowl of tomato soup in front of him. Mom was pouring the last of the contents of the soup pan into a mug for Joey. He liked to drink his soup instead of eat it with a spoon. It was easier to get every last drop that way.

"Mom, can I make some chocolate milk and have it with my soup and sandwich?"

"I'll get you some, but only if you march back up those stairs and run a brush through that hair," Mother demanded.

"Okay," Joey replied as he rushed back up the steps to the bathroom and swatted at his hair a couple of times with a brush. Then he was back at the kitchen table, waiting to say grace. He couldn't wait to break his sandwich in half and dunk it into his chocolate milk. Then he would take the whole drippy gooey bite and shove it into his mouth, a ritual Father always seemed torn about. He had said he thought it was bad manners, but he liked to do it too, so he couldn't really blame the kid for doing it. They had come to an agreement. It would be allowed only when they were alone, and only in the privacy of their own kitchen, nowhere else. If he was caught dunking outside of these four walls, life was to take a drastic turn for the worse. When Joey's soup and sandwich were gone, two glasses of chocolate milk later, Father asked if they could be excused.

"Are you ready, Joe?"

"Ready for what?"

"Ready to see what I have to show you, of course."

"Oh yeah! What is it?" Joey asked excitedly.

"Just follow me." Father and son headed out the back door. Dad led the way to the workshop. As they stepped out the door, Joey was shocked at how cold it had become. Just this afternoon when he'd walked to Nick's house, it had seemed as though spring was all but here. But now, only a couple hours later, Old Man Winter was breathing his icy breath again. He even noticed Father shiver ever so nonchalantly.

"BRRRRRRR!" Joey could see his breath as he spoke. Heck, he could almost watch it freeze as it left his mouth, then crystallize and shatter on impact with the frosty ground below. "Dad, is it going to be warm inside the woodshed?"

"Yeah, Joe. It should be considerably warmer than it is out here. I have a small fire going in the woodstove, so let's put a move on it. What do you say, son?" Dad said as he broke into a slow trot.

"That sounds like a good idea to me," Joey replied as he raced Father to the sultry haven.

"Oh, no you don't," Father called as the little boy streaked past him. He hurried his pace just enough to catch up with the chilled child, and then he edged ahead. He maintained this slight lead right up to the point of touching the door where he performed a very convincing stumble. This allowed Joey to slip past and reach the shed first.

"I win!" Joey shouted as he grabbed the door handle.

"Darned if you aren't getting faster all the time, Joe."

"I think it's from taking Caesar for walks," Joey pontificated. "I have to run really fast to keep up with him." While Joey talked, Dad opened the door and they both stepped inside.

"Well, whatever it is, it seems to be working," Dad complimented as he strode over to the workbench. "Here it is, Joe. The finished product of your strife." Father held out Nick's present, fully stained and shellacked. Joey could see the light caroming off of it, how it sent the rays in different directions each time Dad moved the glimmering token of esteem.

"Wow!" That was the only word Joey could come up with. "Wow!" It was even more perfect than before. It was beautiful. It was the best present he had ever seen, or at least the best one he had ever given. This little boy with the warm heart and the frozen red nose had never been more proud of himself than he was at this very second.

"I take it you approve then?" Dad queried.

"Can we show Mom?" Joey asked.

"Certainly. It's dry enough now. I don't see any reason why we can't take it in and show your mother." Off they went, Joey toting the glossy showpiece like it was made of glass instead of wood. He charged through the back door screaming.

Friends are a
blessing from God

"Mom! Mom! Look at Nicholas's present. Isn't it beautiful? I told you it was perfect. Dad said it was the produce of my life."

"That would be, product of your strife," Dad corrected politely as he rubbed his hands together trying to create some friction and get the blood circulating again.

"Oh, Joey. It's wonderful. I'm sure Nicholas will love it. Now, let me see, what does it say?"

Before she even had time to get a decent look at the lettering, Joey blurted, "Friends are a blessing from God."

"Yes, they are, dear, and Nicholas is truly blessed to have a friend like you give him a present like this."

"I'm blessed, too. 'Cause Nicholas is my friend, and he's going to come to my house for Christmas," Joey boasted.

"Then he said yes?" Mother asked.

"Oh yeah," giggled the absent-minded little boy. "I didn't tell you. He said he couldn't decline such heartfelt generosity. I told him that I would go and get him in the morning. But I gotta open my presents first and then. … Oh! That reminds me, I hafta wrap Nicholas's present. Do we got any wrapping paper and tape? Is it in the closet with the Christmas stuff? I think I can find it. Should I put it in something or just wrap it up like this? Oh yeah, and I need some scissors. I think I have some in my room from school..." The elated youth rambled on, as Mother gathered all the necessities on his list.

"Here you go, dear. Be careful, and clean up your mess. I will be up in a bit to check on you." At that, the precocious juvenile clamored up the stairs to create the perfect shroud for the perfect gift.

Mother sauntered over to Father and kissed him affectionately. "I love you," she intimated.

"What was that for?" he responded. "Whatever I did, let me know what it is, so I can do it again."

"For being a wonderful father and great husband."

"Oh! Is that all?" he quipped playfully. "Well, you and that boy make it real easy, and thank you." With that, he kissed her back.

Upstairs, Joey was putting the final touches on his wrap job. He placed the bow Mother had brought him just to the left of center. It was the bow Mom had made to put on Dad's present last year. It had three loops and a long curly tail, and it was red. Mom saved all the Christmas wrappings. She thought it was a waste to throw away something that someone had put so much thought and effort into. Joey liked to just rip things open, but he was glad Mom had managed to rescue this bow. To conclude, he cut a small square out of one of the leftover scraps and wrote on it: "To Nicholas, from your friend Joey." He taped the label to the package, right next to the frilly bow.

"There. That does it." Just as the final word came out of his mouth, Mother and Father entered.

"Well, Joe, how did it go?" Father inquired.

"I just got it done."

"It looks very attractive, son." Mother complimented.

"How about getting yourself ready for bed there, little man?" Dad more demanded than asked. Joey jumped to his feet and went to the bathroom to brush his teeth and wash his face. Meanwhile, Dad found a good Bible story to read. When Joey returned, Mother tucked him into bed and Father read the story. It was about Jesus and his disciples eating a gigantic feast. It was called the Last Supper, and it talked about how Jesus wanted to live but knew he must die. For that was God's plan. That was pretty much the idea of it from what Joey could understand, which was almost nothing. It was beyond his scope of comprehension. Why did Jesus have to die? When the story was over, Mother and Father kissed him goodnight and turned on the night light on their way out of the room. Joey closed his eyes and began to speak aloud.

"Dear Jesus, I'm sorry you had to die when you didn't want to. I pray for Mommy and Daddy and all of my family and friends. I pray that Uncle Frank will get better real soon, so he can be home for Christmas. Mostly, I pray for Nicholas. He didn't look so good today, and I pray that you will make him feel better. I am glad that he's my friend and Caesar, too. Please be with Santa when he delivers presents to all the good boys and girls, and even some of the not so good ones, too. Amen."

DAY 5:

Wednesday, December 25 (Christmas Day)

On a regular day, if there was one thing Joey could choose not to do, that one thing would be getting up at four-thirty in the morning. He hated it. He'd rather eat two plates of broccoli and go back for seconds on spinach. On a regular day, he would roll over and go back to whatever it was he might have been dreaming about. But, that was on a regular day. This was Christmas morning. And on Christmas morning, getting up before the rooster crowed seemed like a great idea. So that's what he did. As he climbed out of bed and shuffled to his window, he could see the snow falling outside, each tiny flake dancing through the air. They fell one after another; no two were the same, like a frozen water ballet, on a moonlit stage. The street below was silent, not a creature was stirring. But Joey suspected that if it were possible to see that far, he could have spied Bobby and Michael scurrying about in their room as well. But he hadn't dragged himself out of a warm, soft bed just so he could watch the snow fall or spy on his friends. He had a mission, a very secret mission, one that would take extreme cunning and daring to accomplish.

His first move was to make his way to the bedroom door. He reached for the handle. He could feel the hard metal in his palm as he turned the knob ever so slowly. The click of the latch as it cleared the strike plate gave our young secret agent reason to pause. A moment later a muffled creak of the door stopped him again. He listened carefully but heard nothing. Cautiously, he stepped into the hallway, looking first to the right, then to the left. On his right was a single door. The lack of any human-shaped shadow in the glimmer of the bathroom night light signified that all was clear on that front. To the left was where the danger lay. Sixteen feet of carpet had to be traversed to reach the balcony at the top of the stairs. To get there he must pass two doors, one on the left, one on the right. The one to the right posed no real threat; it was only the linen closet. Towels and sheets were the least of his worries at this juncture. But the one on the left, now that was another story. It was the entrance to the enemy stronghold. He must use all of his resources to get by that fortress in tact. One careless misstep and the whole mission could self-destruct before his very eyes. That first step was crucial. The miniature G-man lifted his foot and extended the knee, then silently and gracefully placed his toes on the ground. Like a tiger stalking his prey, he crept down the hallway. But something was wrong; he had the distinct feeling of being watched. A quick survey of his surroundings led him to the source. There on the wall was the portrait of Grandma and Grandpa. Each was sporting a smug, omnipotent grin on their face with the slightest hint of revenge in their eyes. They knew this exercise all too well. They were welcome allies. Having passed the linen closet, only one obstacle remained. Joey skillfully skirted past the antagonistic entryway trying to anticipate even the vaguest sign of enemy arousal. Sensing none, he quickly traveled the final few feet that put him beyond the perilous portal. A heavy sigh, a mischievous grin, a hop, a skip, and a jump were the only things left between our hero and his bonanza. After narrowly escaping the hand of death, or at the very least a severe tongue lashing, the young adventurer took a deserved rest.

As Joey stood there looking out over the setting below, his arms resting on the balcony railing, a smile came to his face. He imagined what it would be like later that day—Mother coming out of the kitchen with her hands full of delicious treats, Father standing in the entryway greeting their guests. There would be Grandma and Grandpa; Great Uncle Steve; Frank's wife, Alice; and their little baby girl. It was sad to think that Uncle Frank wouldn't be able to make it. Aunt Sue should be here, a little late as usual. You can never get anywhere on time when you have to get four children ready and into the car, at least that's what she always said. You never know who else might show up. Then there's the reason he got out of bed in the first place—the living room. Joey cautiously headed for the stairway.

He wasn't sure how old he was when it started, but he knew he'd been doing it for the last two Christmas mornings. He kicked his leg up over the banister and straddled it in an upright position. He sat there for a moment holding onto the huge globe that rested at the head of the railing. He bent over so his belly lay flat against the smooth wood. He kicked out both legs and one, two, three, he let go. Soon he could feel the breeze in his hair. The friction of wool on wood created a burning sensation as he picked up speed. Gravity makes for one heck of a ride. As he neared the bottom, he gripped the rail a bit tighter, then a little tighter still. He timed the slowing process exactly so that just before he ran into the big globe at the end of the banister his momentum was slowed enough to jump off. It was quite an intricate procedure. More than once he'd paid the price for errors in judgment, but repetition is a great teacher. Once his little joy ride was complete and he had both feet firmly on the ground, the essence of the moment engulfed him.

You know those special memories, the ones that are still vivid after twenty years? The ones you look back on and get the feeling that you're living that moment all over again? You can feel the warmth of woolen cowboy and Indian pajamas against your skin. You can feel the rush of adrenalin, because you are about to turn the corner that opens into the world of wonder that is Christmas morning. You see the flicker of candle-light darting from wall to wall, all around the living room: stockings, crammed full of goodies, dangling from little hooks on the mantle over the fireplace; the stacks of presents, those from the night before, and the newly placed ones left by the jolly old man with the gray beard and the red suit; the glow of the moonlight as it makes its way through the open drapes. You hear the birds singing their own brand of Christmas carols in the trees outside the dining room window. These are the memories that fill your heart with excite-ment every time you conjure them. They grip you and take you away so completely that you have to force yourself to realize that it is only your mind's eye and not the real thing. That's what John Adams was experiencing as he watched his son. He turned to his wife and smiled, content in the knowledge that she too felt similar pangs in her heart as she viewed the little boy with the saucer-sized eyes.

"One present!" hollered Father.

"Awww, Dad," Joey moaned. "How can I pick just one?"

"I'm sure you'll find a way, dear," Mother encouraged.

Joey wandered into the living room in a sort of daze. Where had his parents come from? How could they have possibly heard him? Why hadn't he heard them? How long had they been there? Why wasn't he in big trouble? And most perplexing of all, how was he going to choose only one present from the abundance that was spread out in front of him?

"Can I check my stocking first?" he asked optimistically.

"I suppose we could allow that," Father consented.

"Make sure you get it cleaned up when you're through, dear," Mother warned as she and Dad descended the final few steps and started toward the living room.

"I will, Mom," Joey proclaimed as he ran to the fireplace and hoisted the bulging stocking from its roost. He then dropped to the floor and turned it upside down, watching the contents pour to the ground, bouncing and rolling everywhere. There were walnuts and peanuts, hazelnuts, and chocolate-covered cashews. An apple and an orange that rolled under the chair; there were assorted candies and a set of jacks with a little rubber ball. Then in the very bottom of the foot-shaped material, he found three pairs of dress socks and a pencil with his name engraved on it.

"Thank you, Santa!" the little boy with a big smile exclaimed. "Mommy, Daddy, look what I got!" he shouted as he held up the socks and the pencil with "JOEY" etched into the side of it. "Aren't they neat?"

"They sure are, son," Dad stated with a satisfied smile. Meanwhile, Joey was quickly gathering all of the articles of holiday cheer and stashing them back into his stocking. He even remembered to grab the orange from under the chair.

"There! Can I open my present now?"

"Sure you can. Do you know which one you want to tackle yet?" Father asked.

"Hmmmm, let me see." Joey rummaged through the mass of colorfully wrapped boxes, looking for just the right one. Finally, he came across an extremely large package near the wall at the back of the tree. "Is this one mine?"

"Well, look at the tag, sweetie. What does it say?" Mother advised.

"It is! It is mine. J-O-E-Y spells Joey. I wanna open this one."

"Very well then, bring it over here, so we can watch."

"Okay, Mom." With that, the little boy lifted the large box and teetered over to an open area where his parents could see him.

"Who's it from?" Mother asked, knowing full well what the answer was.

"It's from Grandma and Grandpa," Joey replied as he began to tear away the purple wrapping. With shreds of violet paper all around him, he tugged at the flaps on top of the huge brown box. "I can't get it open," he complained.

"Hang on, let me help you," Father offered as he pulled a small knife from his pocket and sliced the tape that ran the length of the cumbersome carton. Almost before the blade was safely back in its cover, the anxious youth had grabbed the package and stripped the tape from the top. He dug into that box like a dog after a bone. It seemed as though half his body had disappeared before Joey exhumed himself from the cardboard container. When he did, he had two things: a gigantic stuffed bear and an even larger smile.

"It's the one from Anderson's Department store. The one I saw when I visited Grandma and Grandpa this summer. Isn't he wonderful?" Joey gasped, still somewhat in shock.

"He certainly is, dear. I think he'll make a great friend," said Mother.

"Indeed he will," Father agreed. "What are you going to name him?"

Joey thought for a moment and then another ear-to-ear grin formed on his face. "I'm going to call him Nicky, 'cause he's going to be a great friend, like Nicholas."

"That sounds like a perfect name for him, dear, and a beautiful sentiment," announced Mother proudly.

"That's real nice of you, son. Now, why don't we get this mess cleaned up so we can start getting ready for sunrise service?"

"All right, Dad. Come on, Nicky, let's get cracking. You helped make this mess, so you can help me clean it up," Joey berated precociously.

For the next forty-five minutes, the entire Adams household preened, primped, and prepared themselves for the early morning worship service. Once everyone was ready, they made their way through the virgin snow to a little church that sat on the corner of Birch and First streets. As they walked, Joey followed in his father's footsteps, literally. Each footprint that Dad left, Joey would follow behind him and step into the same print, or at least he would try to step into it. Dad's strides were so much longer than his that sometimes he would have to jump from one footprint to the next. All the same, it made the walk to the church seem a whole lot shorter. Once inside the sanctuary, they scooted into a pew in the second row. Joey took off his coat and gloves, then leaned back and listened as the preacher started the ceremony. They sang all kinds of Christmas hymns: "Oh Come All Ye Faithful" and "Away in the Manger," "Silent Night," and "What Child is This." These were just a few of the songs they used to celebrate this special day. Then the minister started his sermon. He talked about the birth of Jesus, and how we should all be grateful. He said that the main reason for our gratitude shouldn't be the birth of Jesus; it should be his death, because that's what frees us from our sins. It allows us to release our problems and live a life free from the worries of the world. Joey was starting to under-stand. Maybe that's what he meant when he said

Jesus had to die to make the world better for those who still lived. After another Christmas hymn and the final prayer, Joey and his family filed into the fellowship hall. Bobby and Michael located their young friend at the snack table as he was stashing two cookies into his coat pocket.

"Hey, runt," Bobby called.

"Yeah, runt, what ya doin'?" echoed Michael

"I think we're gettin' ready to leave," replied Joey. "My dad says we have to get home and get stuff ready for dinner."

"Did you already open presents?" quizzed Michael.

"I got to open one, and I got some socks and a pencil with my name on it in my stocking," Joey answered.

"We didn't get to open any of our presents. Our dad made us go back to bed, 'cause we woke him up too early," Bobby complained.

"Bobby, come on, we gotta go," Michael urged. "Dad said we have to be home before it gets too late."

"Too late for what?" Bobby asked.

"I don't know. That's just what he said, so we better get going," Michael replied.

"Okay. Okay," Bobby conceded. "Bye, Joey. See ya later."

"Yeah. Bye, Joey," Michael added just before they slipped out the side door. Joey wandered around the room until he saw his parents chatting with Auntie Alice.

"There you are, Joe. We were just about to come hunt you down. Are you ready to go home and open some of those Christmas presents?" Dad inquired.

"You bet!" the little boy squealed as he grabbed his coat and headed for the door.

"Slow it down, young man," cautioned Father. "This is the Lord's house you know, and there is no running allowed in His house."

"Okay, Dad." Joey slowed to a walk and finally to a complete halt. Mom and Dad soon caught up, and they all trudged through the snowy tundra back to the house.

When everyone was inside, Father started a fire in the fireplace. As the heat from the blaze warmed the house, he began to muddle through the mass of presents. He sorted each one according to who it was for. There was a small mound for Grandma and Grandpa, a slightly larger one for Mom and Dad, and a rather large stack for Joey. Then there was another pile for everyone else.

"All right then, let's get started." Dad's voice was like the recess bell at school. It set off some kind of release mechanism in Joey's brain, and the rest of the world just kind of disappeared. For the next few minutes, Joey went into a gift opening frenzy. He could hardly remember one present from the next. All that seemed to matter was that there was another one left to tear into. Forget about saving the paper; forget about reusing the container; sure, you might be able to salvage a bow here or there, but for the most part, it was a flurry of hands and arms; a barrage of battered boxes and ripped wrappings; a veritable tornado of tattered tissue. When the storm was over, the little boy was left with a pile of clothing, a pad of writing paper, a collection of toys, and a huge mess.

"Are you about through?" Father questioned with a stunned look. He was sure this feeling should have passed by now. The rampage occurred each Christmas, but for some inconceivable reason, it shocked him every year.

"Is that all?" asked Joey.

"Clean up your mess, dear." Mother giggled. She didn't know if she was laughing at the question, the commotion, or the expression on her husband's face, but she was certain of one thing: this is what Christmas morning was supposed to be like.

"When you've finished doing what your mother told you to do, we'll see if there's anything else," Dad reported, trying to hide the cat-that-ate-the-canary smile that had blossomed on his face.

"Dad, what did you get?" Joey inquired as he stuffed a large wad of colored paper into the garbage can he'd garnered from the kitchen.

"I got a nice shirt and tie from Grandma, and some very cool tools from your mom."

"What did you get, Mommy?"

"I received a pair of beautiful earrings from your father, and a new Bible from Grandma and Grandpa. Don't the earrings look spectacular, dear?" She flaunted as she held her hair back to show them off.

"They sure do, Mom," Joey agreed adamantly. "Is this clean enough?" he asked in a hopeful voice.

"Take all of your new clothes upstairs and put them away and maybe I'll make some hot eggnog with cinnamon," said Mom.

"Eggnog! I'm on my way." Joey rushed upstairs. His journey wasn't as swift as it might have been, though. He had to stop three times to pick up different articles of clothing that he'd dropped. Sometimes being in a hurry only makes it take longer.

In the meantime, Dad snuck into the hallway closet and rolled out a new bicycle. It was red with a blue seat. It had two white stripes down each side and red, white, and blue streamers dangling from the handlebar grips. But best of all, it had a bell; a silver bell that shined so brightly you could see your reflection in it. There was a small lever on the left-hand side, and when you pushed it, the bell would ring. The noise it made was kind of like the sound change makes as it jingles in your pocket while you run, only louder. This bike, or one an awful lot like it, had been at the very top of Joey's Christmas list, the one he'd given Santa last weekend. It may well have been the coolest bike in all of Vermont, at least that's what Joey was thinking as he entered the living room. He couldn't get over the way it glimmered in the candlelight, how the flames seemed to lick the new paint then dance away. Joey just stood there and stared. The look on his face didn't require a picture. It was one his parents would remember for the rest of their lives. Mouth wide open, eyes speaking the words his tongue couldn't express, lips pursing into a smile that covered his tiny face like shadows on a crescent moon. It was just one more clipping in the photo album of memories stored in frames that hung in the back of their collective minds.

"So? What do you think?" Dad queried. "Would this count as anything else?"

"It's just what I wanted!" Joey shrieked. "Oh, Mommy and Daddy, it's perfect. Thank you! Thank you! Can I ride it?

"Not in the house," Father joked. "Take it outside, son, and be real careful 'cause it's starting to snow.

"First, go upstairs and put some warm clothes on," Mom warned.

Joey raced up the stairs to his room. He ransacked his drawers and closet for winter clothes and put on the rubber boots he'd gotten from Granny Jones last Christmas. He reappeared at the base of the stairs looking more like a scarecrow than a little boy ready for a bike ride.

"Well, that ought to keep ya warm." Dad laughed.

"Put your coat and gloves on," Mom added. "If you have any room left, that is."

"No problem, Mom." Joey added the final accessories to his outerwear ensemble, grabbed his new bike, and headed out the door. "Bye, Mom and Dad." He was off. His parents watched out the front window as Joey made figure eight patterns in the driveway. They proudly followed his tracks as he cruised up and down the sidewalk between the house and the end of the block. Mother's heart skipped a beat when she saw the back end of that new two wheeler start to slide as her baby boy rounded the corner, heading up the walk towards the house. Joey was quick, though. He caught himself with his left foot, pushed the bike back into an upright position, and calmly glided to a halt at the front door. At this point, he quickly climbed off and carefully propped his new treasure on its kickstand, then hurried into the house.

"Mom, Dad, can I go to Nicholas's house now? I want to ask him if he wants to come over. I have to take him his present anyway."

"I suppose that'd be okay. Make sure he knows we won't be eating until this afternoon, and don't be a bother," Mother cautioned as Joey put on his winter coat. "And hurry back. We have other guests coming, and there's still a lot to do before everyone gets here. We're going to need some help from a strong young man, and I think you know who I mean."

"Okay, Mom. I'll just take him his present and then come right home." Joey did an about face and raced out the front door.

Almost immediately, the door flew open again and the little boy in the multi-layered clothing rushed back in.

"Oops! I forgot the present," Joey declared with a giggle. Mom and Dad just laughed as he raced up the stairs and back down again, then out the door he went. He picked up his bike, stashed the gift into the inner depths of his upper attire, hopped on, and pedaled off to Nick's house.

There are few things that compare to the feeling you get when you take that first real journey on a brand new bicycle. The exhilaration of the wind in your face as you virtually fly through the streets of town. The sense of freedom you get as you pump your legs faster and faster, and then lift your feet from the pedals and coast down Hill Street like an eagle soaring across the sunlit sky. This is one of the great joys of youth. With one gift, a fifteen-minute walk turned into a three-minute ride. Well, it would have lasted three minutes if Joey hadn't taken every back road between his house and Nicholas's. As it was, it still took about fifteen minutes, but it sure didn't seem that long. It's easy to think, or not to think for that matter, when you're on the road. Riding along, you can let your mind go. All of those repressed feelings seem to come forward, inching closer and closer to the front of your brain with each revolution of the tires. A revolution revelation you might call it. Whatever else it might be, it certainly is therapeutic. As Joey churned his way up the long steep drive to the house, he started to think about Nicholas's present. He was sure to like it.

Joey's thoughts were interrupted by the feeling of fatigue that had taken over his legs and the rest of his body. He couldn't remember being this tired after walking halfway up this hill, but riding had taken every ounce of energy he had. He willed his body onward. Harder and harder, he pedaled until he couldn't go any farther. At first he felt bad that he hadn't made it to the top; it seemed like somehow he'd failed. But that emotion changed after he climbed off the bike. He took a moment to get his legs under him and then turned to face the nemesis that had beaten him. Surveying the landscape, he saw the way the driveway wound up the hill. He noticed how it got steeper the nearer you got to the top. He could also see the rest of town, all the back streets he had taken in getting to this point, and suddenly he felt a whole lot better. He even thought that maybe he deserved a rest for making it as far as he had, so he sat down on one of the large rocks that lined the drive to the big house. He looked down on the little village and saw it from a perspective that was extremely intuitive, even for the most mature of seven-year-olds. He gazed out across the snow-covered streets and yards. He saw the Christmas lights and the street lights. He saw kids on new sleds sliding and screaming with joy. He saw a cloud-filled sky. He saw the touch of God's hand. And he saw it all, each and every picture that ran through his brain, through the eyes of a child. He said, "Thank you, God," and somehow felt stronger.

He picked up his bicycle and pushed it the last twenty yards to the top of the driveway. He parked it next to the huge stone pillar at the edge of the porch, walked to the door, and rang the bell. He stood there for what seemed like a long time and then rang the bell again. Something was wrong. What was it? Oh yeah! The present. He'd forgotten that he'd put it inside his coat somewhere. Just as he fished it out, he heard Caesar barking inside the house. Shortly after that, he heard the lock click and the latch turn as Nicholas opened the door.

"Merry Christmas, young man," Nicholas stated, somewhat winded.

"Merry Christmas to you, Nicholas," Joey responded. "Are you ready to come to my house for dinner?"

"Is it that time already?" the old man asked.

"Nah. We won't be eating till this afternoon, but I was just wonderin' if you wanted to come over now, since I was here," Joey said hopefully.

"I'm afraid I'm not prepared to make that trip just yet, Joey. Maybe I could just meet you at your house? You said it should start at about two o'clock, isn't that correct?

"Yeah. About then."

"Then I shall see you there," Nicholas confirmed.

"Okay. It's 124 Elm Street. You promise you'll come?" Joey asked.

"I promise," Nicholas vowed. "Now, what is that you have behind you're back?"

"It's your present," Joey exclaimed. "I told you I made you one, remember? Oh yeah, and my dad helped."

"As a matter of fact, I do recall something about a gift. What is it?" Nick questioned playfully.

"I can't tell you. Then it wouldn't be a surprise," Joey parried.

"Well, the suspense is killing me. Can I open it yet?"

"Sure you can." The little boy handed his friend the carefully wrapped package. The old man took it and admired it for a moment.

"You did a nice job wrapping it."

"Thank you. My mom saved the bow from last year."

"Well, it looks very nice." Nicholas's heart was beating a little faster now, surprisingly so. He hadn't had this kind of anticipation about a gift since before Gladdys died. But now frustration was setting in as well. His fingers weren't working like they were supposed to. He couldn't get the paper to tear.

"Why don't you tear the bow off for me, so I can save it?" Nicholas held out the package so that Joey could pull the bow off and in the process tear the paper. "Thank you, young man." That done, he continued where Joey had left off.

Joey watched as the old man ripped the last of the colored tissue from the glazed placard. Nicholas's face went blank as he read the words out loud: "Friends are a blessing from God" Joey wondered what was wrong. Then he saw a tear trickle down the cheek of that blank face.

"What's the matter? Don't you like it?" the naive little boy asked.

Nicholas wiped the tears away and answered. "It's beautiful, Joey. It is the most honest, caring, and sensitive gift I think anyone has ever given me, with the possible exception of my wife. Thank you so very much, and thank your father, too." Just then, Nicholas stumbled and only barely caught himself. Joey made a move to help but backed away as Nick erected himself.

"Are you all right?"

"I am fine. I just need to rest before I take that walk to your house. You run along home, help your parents get everything ready, and I'll see you in a while."

"All right. See you soon. Caesar can come, too. Bye, Nicholas."

"Good-bye." The old man bid the little boy adieu. Then he quietly shut the door, looked down at his hands, and gazed at his new holiday memory. *What an amazing young man,* he thought as he awkwardly made his way back down the long hall to the den.

Joey was on a cloud, floating through the air on his new bike. Not literally floating, mind you, but he was feeling pretty good. Nicholas loved his present. It had made him cry. Joey had never given a present that made someone cry before. His parents must have known what they were talking about when they said that making a present from the heart was better than buying one from the store. Of course, if he'd had the foresight to realize it, he would have noticed that his parents were right about a whole lot of things, but that just isn't something that seven-year-old boys do. They are much more interested in things like building snowmen, riding bikes, playing with toys, and eating Christmas dinner. It was always great when everyone came to their house to eat because when they did, they brought more presents; now that is something that a kid can get interested in, even excited about. Joey felt the pedals on his bicycle circle more quickly as these thoughts raced through his head. A couple of minutes later, he was parking his bike in the backyard and scurrying up the steps to the back entrance.

As soon as the door slammed shut, Joey could hear the sound of a familiar voice in the dining room. At first, he wasn't sure whose it was, but when the bell of recognition rang in the back of his brain, it sent a signal to his mouth and a huge smile formed. It was a smile that didn't just stop at his face; it spread throughout his body like lemonade filling a glass of ice. It was a very satisfying smile.

"Uncle Frank! Uncle Frank!" Joey's pace hurried to a run as he entered the dining room. He sprinted the last fifteen feet, wrapped his little arms around Frank's waist, and proceeded to give one of his patented "Joey" hugs, at which point Uncle Frank's lemonade glass filled rapidly.

"I thought you weren't going be here," said Joey as he squeezed a little tighter. Then he peered up at Uncle Frank with a confused, yet ecstatic look on his face.

"Hey, little buddy. I wasn't sure I was going to be here either, but they let me out early, for good behavior. It sure is good to see your smiling face, Joey." Frank was on the verge of tearing up, but caught himself and changed the subject. "So when do we eat around this place, anyways?"

"Dinner should be ready around two o'clock, Frank," Mother announced cheerfully, "but there are plenty of snacks and drinks on the table and more in the kitchen when those are gone."

That was all Joey needed to hear. In seconds he was at the table gathering up some of Mom's delicious pumpkin rolls and a glass of cold eggnog. He sat down on the love seat at the back side of the room next to the Christmas tree. As he ate, drank, and listened, he began to think about the wonder of this time of year. This was something he had never done before. He watched as Great Uncle Steve and Aunt Jill arrived. He saw the way that Mom's face lit up as she kissed their cheeks and made them feel welcome. He looked around the room and noticed how everyone not only seemed to be happy, but actually was happy. He could see it in their eyes. Why he hadn't recognized all of this before was a mystery. But then again, there were a lot of things different about this Christmas. He couldn't explain it. He just knew that there was something very special about this day. Soon, Grandma and Grandpa were there. A little later, Aunt Sue showed up with all four kids in tow. She made her usual apologies and hollered a few well-placed phrases about silence being golden and peace being a major factor in the whole Christmas experience. Mom kissed her cheek as well. She hugged each of the children and talked about how much they'd grown and how adorable they were. Then Mother excused herself to the kitchen while everyone else mingled and chatted. Joey and the four little people hung around the tree, trying to figure out how many new presents had arrived and who they were for. Two for Timmy, two for Sara, and three for Joey; the other kids were too little to truly appreciate the number of gifts they received.

It seemed to Joey that time must have been in a hurry, because the next thing he knew, Mom was calling everyone into the dining room for dinner.

"But Mom, Nicholas isn't here yet," Joey wailed. "He said he would be here for dinner. I told him it was at two o'clock. Is it two o'clock yet?"

"Yes, dear, it's about five after, but I'm sure Nicholas will be here. He probably had to stop somewhere along the way. You run upstairs and get washed up and then we'll eat. If he isn't here by the time we're done, you can ride your bike over and get him. I'll keep his plate warm."

"But Mom—" Joey started to argue.

"Son, you heard your mother, now get upstairs and wash up," Father interrupted.

"Okay, I'm going," Joey huffed as he shuffled off to the bathroom. He wondered sometimes why he bothered to argue with his parents at all. He never won. There were two of them and only one of him, so the deck was always stacked against him. Such is the nature of adolescence. Joey washed his hands and face and then trotted back downstairs and took his place at the table between Mom and Uncle Frank.

The dinner table was overflowing with food—ham, turkey, stuffing, sweet potatoes, salads of all kinds. There were fresh-baked rolls, cranberry sauce, gravy, and a whole extra table filled with tantalizing desserts.

"This looks incredible," gushed Aunt Sue. Then a murmur of unanimous agreement spread around the table.

"It truly looks delicious, dear," Father stated in admiration. "Shall we eat?"

"Darling, would you be kind enough to say grace for us?" Mother asked with a caring stare in Father's direction.

"Certainly. Dear Heavenly Father, we are so grateful for all the blessings you gladly cast upon us. We pray for understanding and patience in the times that we feel uncertain of your plan. We do know that you will provide, even in ways we cannot comprehend. Mostly Lord, we thank you for the friends and family gathered here today on this holy day. (*Except not Nicholas,* Joey thought). We pray that you will bless our bodies with this elaborate feast given in honor of your son, and may your will be done. It is in his name that we pray. AMEN."

DAY 5:
Wednesday, December 25 (Christmas Afternoon)

Joey was in a state of confusion. Although he was thoroughly enjoying his dinner, part of him didn't feel like eating at all. It was really great to have Uncle Frank and all of the people he loved so much there to share in the fundamental nature of what Christmas is supposed to be about. Still, without Nicholas, something was missing. He couldn't wait to open the rest of his presents, yet he wanted to leave right away to find out what was keeping his friend. Back and forth his emotions swung like the pendulum in the old grandfather clock that sat in the window of Baker's Drug Store. As time ticked on, everyone managed to get in one last bite of apple pie before hitting the breaking point between *it tastes sooo good* and *I couldn't eat another bite.*

"May I be excused now, please, and can I go and find out how come Nicholas isn't here yet?" Joey asked politely.

"Yes, dear, you may," Mother consented. "Be sure and tell Nicholas that dinner is waiting, no matter when he arrives."

"Thank you, Mom. I will."

Joey rushed up to his room and put on his winter coat, then hurried back down the stairs and out the backdoor to his bike. He hopped on, put the pedals in motion, and he was off. As he rode, a strange emotion crept in on him. It seemed to be anger, disappointment, anxiety, and concern all rolled into one. He almost felt sick to his stomach. He wondered if maybe Nicholas had fallen asleep and hadn't woken up yet. Or maybe he couldn't find their house. Joey would have to keep his eyes peeled for any sign of him walking, which shouldn't be too hard since Caesar would be pretty difficult to miss. He refused to believe that he'd just forgotten. It was definitely some-thing else. All of this thinking and wondering had certainly gotten him worked up, so upset in fact, that he hadn't even noticed that he'd ridden his bike all the way to the top of the winding driveway. Adrenalin is a miraculous thing. He parked his bike at the foot of the porch stairs then ran to the door and knocked on it as hard as he could, then he waited. He could hear Caesar bark, but it wasn't getting any closer, so he rang the doorbell. He waited some more. Still Caesar was barking and still not any closer. That mixed emotion sick feeling was quickly turning into fear and panic. Joey started banging on the front door with both fists and screaming Nicholas's name.

"Nicholas! Nicholas! Nicholas!" Joey heard Caesar coming down the long hall. *Finally, Nicholas is awake,* he thought. But when Caesar arrived at the other side of the door, Joey heard a whine that made his heart drop. He had heard Caesar whine for dinner. He'd heard him whine to go outside. He'd heard him whimper because he wanted to play. But this, this was different. This was a cry of pain and suffering, this whine went straight to the heart. Something was wrong.

"Caesar? What is it, boy? Is something wrong?" came the scared little boy's response.

Then Joey heard Caesar barking back down the hall. He ran around the house to the little window where he'd first seen the old man and his companion together. The memory of that moment raced through his head. The vision of Caesar in the window, fangs exposed, scaring him, Bobby, and Michael out of their minds followed shortly thereafter.

But now, there was only the old man lying limp in his chair; Caesar licking his hand and nudging his leg with his nose. On the floor, by the right front leg of the large cushioned chair, Joey saw a handkerchief covered with red stains.

Whatever adrenalin that had carried him up that steep drive was now multiplied by fifty. Everything was a blur. The next thing that Joey could remember was slamming the front door open and screaming with tears streaming.

"Mommy! Daddy! Something's wrong with Nicholas! I tried. ... I knocked on the door ... I yelled his name ... Caesar barked. ... He wouldn't wake up." The little boy collapsed.

"Okay. Okay. It's all right, Joe. It's all right," Father comforted.

"No, it's not all right," Joey cried. "There was a handkerchief..." He couldn't go on. At this point, the whole world sort of became dark. Joey could make out shapes and sounds, familiar words, but nothing made any sense. It was as if everything else was spinning (like a dog chasing his tail), but he was sitting still. He heard something about a patrolman and getting Doc Wilson, but other than that, it was black and dizzy.

"Joey? Are you all right, dear?" asked Aunt Sue.

"Huh?" Joey replied. "Oh. Uh. I don't know. Everything is kinda weird. What's going on?"

"Your mom and dad went to get Doc Wilson, and then they were going to that big house on the hill," answered Sue.

"Nicholas! I gotta go and see if he's okay. I gotta help. Caesar won't let anyone else in the house," Joey rambled.

"We'd better let him go. He makes a good point," Aunt Alice recommended.

"You go ahead and go, Joey. Your mom and dad will be there soon," stated Grandpa.

In seconds, Joey was running out the door and headed for Nicholas's. He didn't even stop to get his bike. In the confusion of it all, he'd actually forgotten he had a bike. He was much too worried about what was going on at Nicholas's house. All talk about Joey not being as fast as the other boys became a myth as he churned through the streets of town toward the Brandon mansion. Before he had time to realize what he was thinking or doing, he was at the base of the hill and on his way up. As he reached the top of the driveway, Joey saw his mother, his father, and Doc Wilson on the front walk. A patrolman was pacing the side of the house looking for an alternate entrance. The front was impassible, due to the presence of Caesar, the huge white wolfhound. Joey reached the porch just as the patrolman suggested they call the vet to "tranquilize the thing."

"No! Wait! He'll let me in! He's my friend!" Joey screamed.

"Give it a shot, son. We've got nothing to lose at this point." The patrolman gave way.

"Except my son's life," Father spoke up.

"Don't worry, Dad. It'll be okay. Caesar wouldn't hurt me." Come to think of it, the dog had stopped barking the moment the boy shouted. Maybe this child could tame the beast; maybe he was just what they needed to get inside.

"Caesar. It's me, boy. Joey. I'm coming in with my mom and dad to see what's wrong with Nicholas."

Joey pulled the key out from under the welcome mat and opened the front door. When he looked inside, Caesar was halfway down the hall.

"It's okay now! Caesar's calmed down! I'm going to check on Nicholas!" Joey hollered back as he headed after his canine comrade.

Mother, Father, and the rest of the group followed. A few seconds later, they were peering through the open door of the den. Looking inside, they saw the old man lying in the large cushioned chair with the huge white dog at his side. Caesar licked the peaceful patriarch's hand and put his head across the arm of the chair. Joey was on the other side of the chair with his face buried in the old man's chest muttering, "Wake up, Nicholas! Wake up, Nicholas!" over and over under his breath. Mary Adams swooped down on her little boy like an angel of mercy from above. She wanted to console him and protect him from one of life's greatest pains. She peeled him from Nicholas's bosom and escorted him off to the fireplace so she could hold him. Caesar followed and licked Joey's cheek. He, too, put his loving touch upon the emotionally tattered child. Doc Wilson was checking Nicholas's vital signs. Dad was wearing a path in the carpet between the chair and the fireplace. Mom was nurturing. Caesar was lying on the Oriental rug next to the tree stump table, licking his paws and glancing back and forth between Nicholas and Joey. And Joey, well, Joey was crying, mostly. His face hurt from trying to hold back the pain of losing his friend. He didn't have to be told that Nicholas was dead; he knew it. Even though he was only seven, he could still recognize the look in Doc Wilson's eyes as he tended to his patient. The way they went blank as he held the stethoscope to Nick's chest. He could see the saddened expression on Dad's face as he told his son that everything was going to be okay.

Caesar knew that his companion was gone, as well. He'd sensed it early that morning. When he'd wanted to go outside to take his morning walk, Nicholas hadn't budged. He'd known it was over when Joey left that morning. He'd seen the way Nicholas had struggled to get back to the den. He'd heard the life leave his body with each cough. He'd watched as the blood-stained handkerchief dropped to the floor. Was he sad? Sure. Was he relieved? Definitely. The pain had lasted way too long. The past four days had brought more joy than he'd ever seen in the old man. An air of inner peace had come over Nick since Joey had come into his life. It was as if all those old feelings of anger, anguish, grief, and guilt had been cleansed, and all of the old business had been taken care of. The time was right to end the physical pain now that the mental was gone. It was time to go and be with Gladdys. Still, Caesar felt for Joey, his newfound friend. It wasn't fair to put someone so young through this kind of grief. How was that little boy to understand? And how would he ever know how much he had done? One thing was certain: Caesar would gladly spend the rest of his life repaying the debt.

It was an odd feeling, incredible, but odd. The way everything was quiet, even though he could sense the activity around him. The light was unbelievably brilliant, yet there was no glare, no distortions, no distractions of any kind. It was peaceful here; not just quiet, it was calm. There was no worry, no doubt, no anger, no confusion, just joy. The air was light and easy to breathe. He felt weightless, like floating on a cloud. Suddenly, Nicholas felt a pull, like gravity, only it was the opposite. It was anti-gravity. He could see himself in the chair, but he was getting further and further away until all he could see was the dazzling light and all he could feel was joy. Somewhere in the distance he heard Gladdys's voice, and he smiled. It was a smile that would last an eternity.

John Adams was at a loss. He felt helpless. There was nothing he could do to help Doc Wilson. Mother was taking care of Joey. What else could he do? He walked. As he walked, he looked. He stared in amazement at all of the grandeur: the expensive paintings, the huge fireplace, the priceless Oriental rug, the abundance of books, the carvings, and the magnificent marble mantle. It was all so unreal to him. As he admired these surroundings, he settled on the mantle and its treasures. He found the purple box with the gold coin in it. The box was open to display the shining heirloom inside. But his focus was taken away. It was drawn to something even more valuable. Directly behind the purple satin covered container was a glazed piece of wood with the heartfelt words: *FRIENDS ARE A BLESSING FROM GOD* on it. Tears came to his eyes as he imagined the sequence of events that placed that ornamentation in that particular location. How hard must it have been? How much devotion did it take for this dying man to use the final breaths of his life to put Joey's present there? He truly was a friend and surely a blessing from God.

"Mommy, Nicholas is dead isn't he?" were the first words Joey had spoken since his mother had rescued him to the fireplace. His voice was void of any real feeling. His heart was numb. It felt like his hand did after he'd slept with it under his pillow all night. It had that annoying tingling sensation, only there was no way to shake the feeling back into his heart.

"My heart hurts, Mommy."

"I know, dear," was all she could say.

"Is Nicholas gone to heaven?"

"Yes, honey. I'm sure he is."

"I don't want him to go to heaven yet. I want him to come and eat dinner at my house. I want everyone to see him play with Caesar. He's nice. He's my friend.

"I know, dear."

"Joe, it's time to go home now," Father broke in.

"Can Caesar come with us? I told Nicholas that Caesar could come to our house."

"Sure he can, son." Father was glad to oblige.

"I'll get his leash," Joey replied, still with no real emotion in his voice.

"I'll take care of everything here folks. You run along," Doc Wilson offered.

"Thanks, Doc. Let me know if there's anything I can do," Father responded.

"I will. And I know it might not seem possible right now, but have a Merry Christmas."

"You too, Doc. You too." John Adams knew that it wasn't going to be easy, but he held out hope that a Merry Christmas could still be had.

Joey was already three quarters of the way down the hall with Caesar in tow by the time Mom and Dad reached the doorway leading out of the den. Actually, Caesar was doing the towing, and Joey's greatest hope was that wherever Caesar wished to go would lead to his house. Caesar's main objective was to make sure Joey got what he wanted.

Time is a fickle thing. It has many variables: emotion, energy, state of mind, reality, fantasy, fate, and weather, right down to what type of measuring device you use. All of these things and many more can influence the way it passes. Joey had run the entire gamut these past few days.

These trips to and from Nicholas's house had been painfully diverse. This excursion seemed to include everything. Caesar's rapid pace made the time move quickly. The deep seated pain of loss made it slow. The lack of understanding made it disappear. Anxiety made it spin. Fear made it race. Fatigue made it drag. The truth of the matter was that Joey had no clue how long the jaunt from the mansion on the hill to the little house on Elm Street had taken. What he did know was that it felt good to be home. Maybe it didn't feel good exactly, but it was comfortable. There's a lot to be said for comfort.

The little boy and the dog shuttled through the front door, passed the wondering crowd, then up the stairs to Joey's room. Blank stares abounded as the gallery watched, only to be broken by the sound of footsteps on the front porch. Mother and Father entered to a barrage of questions.

Joey was oblivious to the commotion in the living room. He was still in a state of shock. His brain was full, his knees were weak, his emotions were spent, his heart was broken, and his life seemed meaningless. His faith was being tested. How could God allow this to happen? He tried so hard to be good and to do what he was told. He honored his mother and father. He loved Jesus. He believed in God. He respected his elders. He loved his neighbors. He made every effort to be nice to people and be polite. He never stole anything. He never even really lied. Maybe a little one here or there to stay out of trouble or to save someone pain. He said his prayers every night. He did his best to be what God wanted him to be. So why would his loving Lord take away the best friend he'd ever had? Why would he make it hurt so bad?

Lying there on his bed, Joey could feel the tears coming. What he couldn't do was stop them. Caesar, curled up on the floor below, sensed the young boy's pain. He'd been through this process before. It didn't make it any easier, and there still weren't any answers. All he could do was stand, put his head on his friend's chest, and lick the teardrops from his cheeks.

"I love you, Caesar!" These were the first words with any real emotion that Joey had spoken since he'd discovered Nicholas. Joey put his hand on the huge beast's head and stroked his nose. Caesar scooted a little closer as his pal scratched behind his ears until he was close enough to get one of Joey's special hugs. It wasn't actually the physical squeeze that was so special. It was the deep emotion behind it that bestowed that unique Joey affection.

Downstairs, Mom and Dad were still fielding inquiries about the afternoon tragedy. How did it happen? When did it happen? Did he have any family? What was going to happen now? And finally, who was going to get all of that money? The standard answer to all of these questions was pretty much the same. They didn't know.

"What was that thing that came in with little Joe?" asked Uncle Frank.

"That would be Caesar," answered Father. "I believe he's a wolfhound of some kind. All I know is that he sure loves our little boy. We never would have gotten into the house if Joe hadn't shown up. As soon he got there, that animal calmed down completely. It was almost as if he'd been waiting for him."

"Did Doctor Wilson say anything?" Grandma asked.

"As a matter of fact, he did," announced Mother. "He said to have a Merry Christmas. And that may be the best advice anyone could give. Why don't we go ahead and finish what we came here for? To celebrate the birth of our Savior and enjoy time with our loved ones."

"What about Joey?" Sara asked.

"I'll run up and see how he's doing," Father said as he headed for the stairs.

The image John Adams witnessed when he opened his son's bedroom door was sublime. Joey was curled up on the floor with his head perched upon the huge white canine like a fluffy down pillow. The happy hound didn't seem to mind. Joey was lying on his side with one little arm tucked under the dog's belly and the other draped over his neck. Caesar's tail wagged in time to the little boy's breathing. When the dog sensed the man walking toward him, he lifted his head and stared.

Those deep blue eyes seemed to look right into John Adams's soul. It was an eerie feeling. As he returned the gaze, he could feel the compassion. He sensed that this animal knew what was going on. What's more, it was doing its best to make the situation better.

"How's he doing, boy?" the man asked, fully expecting an answer.

Caesar's barking response caused Joey to stir and then wake. The youth rubbed his eyes and spoke.

"What's the matter, boy?" Then he saw his father and gave him a half-hearted smile, which was all the heart he had left at this point, so even that took a huge amount of effort.

"Hey there, Joe. How ya doin?"

"Okay, I guess. I feel funny. Not funny funny, weird funny."

"That's understandable. We're going to go ahead and open presents and have some more pie, if you'd like to join us. We'd forgive you if you didn't feel like it, though," Father said as he ran his fingers through his son's hair.

"I think that would be a good idea," Joey replied. "Just 'cause I feel sad doesn't mean everybody else shouldn't have a Merry Christmas. I think Nicholas would want us all to be happy and celebrate Christmas. Can Caesar come and help me open presents?"

"You bet! As a matter of fact, I would guess that there just might be a big ole hambone down there with his name on it. After all, he is an invited guest." With that, the man winked at the dog. It was an odd thing for him to do. He'd never been one for giving human characteristics to pets, but something about this animal compelled him to do that very thing. It may have been the way the dog had looked at him when he entered the room. Or the way it had comforted Joey at the mansion. Maybe it was the emotion of the circumstance and the season. All things aside, it still seemed very unnatural.

Caesar's response confirmed the man's behavior even more: the dog winked back and then lapped his tongue across Joey's face as if to say, "How right you are, my friend." The precocious little boy stood and patted the furry canine's head then walked across the room and out the door. Caesar followed.

Father stood there and watched as the caravan passed. There were no words to describe the pride he felt. His little man was a constant source of inspiration and wonder. As for the dog, he wasn't going there.

Joey and Caesar trotted down the stairs and into the living room. All of those concerned faces staring at him made Joey even more uncomfortable.

"I'm okay," he stated assuredly. "Let's open presents now. Come on, Dad, we're ready."

As those words were spoken, he saw the expressions change. Smiles flashed across the room like a meteor shower on a clear winter night. *Maybe this could be a Merry Christmas after all,* thought John Adams as he watched the transformation.

"Anyone for pie?" Father asked. "Oh, Mother, is there an oversized hambone in the kitchen for our most recent guest?"

"You know, I believe there is." She went to the kitchen to fetch the dog a bone.

As she grabbed the bag out of the refrigerator, she remembered Nicholas's dinner in the oven. She turned the knob to off and pulled the warm plate from inside. While dumping the contents into the garbage pail, she stopped to wonder. What kind of person was this old man? What was it about him that made her baby boy so genuinely fond of him? It made her sad to think that she would never know the answers to these questions. What she did know was that Joey had a gift for finding people with extreme kindness and compassion. He had an even greater gift of being able to make these traits flourish in those people. So whatever it was about the old man, the fact that he had touched her son so deeply would be enough to satisfy this pondering of her heart. As she washed the dish and tucked it into the drain rack, it occurred to her that maybe a part of Nicholas had made it here for Christmas after all, the part that was forever etched upon the life of her little boy.

Joey was showing off the new baseball glove he'd received from Alice and Frank when Mom entered with Caesar's present.

"Here ya go, boy. Merry Christmas!" Mother wished cheerfully as she set the hambone in front of the gentle giant.

Opening presents is always a special thing. It manifests itself in different ways for different people. Children love the anticipation and excitement of something new. Grown-ups appreciate the thought behind the gift, the fact that someone cared enough to share a part of themselves, either emotionally or monetarily. The more mature individuals get to experience what Joey had come to realize. The best part of opening presents was the joy of giving. All around the room, Joey could see the varied ways that his family and friends demonstrated these feelings. One thing was evident: Christmas was alive and well in the Adams household.

Joey was sure that the joy of Christmas was bubbling somewhere deep inside of him as well. It was like soda pop when you shake it up, only he couldn't seem to get the top off of his bottle. The doubts and pain of losing Nicholas were still too fresh. One major question kept running through his mind. Why? Why did Nicholas have to die? Why did God take him away? Why did it have to hurt so much? Why couldn't he understand?

The doorbell gave Joey quite a start. Once he realized what it was, he got to his feet and went to the door. He opened it to the sight of Doc Wilson standing there with a genuine smile and holding a large bag.

"Merry Christmas, young man. How are you doing?"

"I'm good," Joey replied, not wanting his mixed feelings to spoil Christmas for anyone else.

"What ya got in the bag?"

"Just a few things I gathered up," Doc answered.

"Mom, Dad, Doc Wilson is here, and I think he brought presents!" hollered Joey as he stared at the bag. He couldn't seem to take his eyes off of it. It wasn't so much a bag as a sort of woven cloth sack. It was red and had a picture of Santa Clause on it. But what kept the little boy's attention wasn't really the color or the picture; it was more the way it bulged at the seams.

"Come on in, Doc. We were just opening presents and having pie. You want some? Mom, can Doc Wilson have some pie?" Joey rambled on as he began to get caught up in excitement of the moment. When he turned around, he almost ran into his mother, who was coming into the foyer from the living room.

"Most certainly," she replied in her most sincere happy-to-see-you voice. "Please join us, Doc. We've got pie, eggnog, and leftovers."

"Well, maybe just a piece of pie. The little lady is waiting at home. I told her I wouldn't be too long."

"You want me to carry the bag for you, Doc?" Joey offered.

"Joey, this bag is almost as big as you are," Doc warned.

"I can handle it," the anxious youth stated confidently as he reached for the sack.

"Very well, have a go at it then," conceded Doc as he gave up the cumbersome pack.

Joey graciously accepted the responsibility, though he had to admit it was partly for selfish reasons. He wanted to see what was inside. That seven-year-old curiosity had kicked in again. His mind was racing with thoughts of what it might be.

"Hello, Doc." Dad stood up and shook Doc Wilson's hand. "How did everything go?"

"It went well. We got the old guy all taken care of. It's nice to see you folks moving forward."

"Yeah, we got some pretty good advice, so we decided to take it," Father responded with a smile.

"Here you are, Doc," Mother stated as she handed him a warm piece of apple pie, a glass of eggnog, and a fork.

"Thank you, dear lady. It looks absolutely delicious. Oh! By the way, Nicholas's lawyer came by while we were getting everything together. He said he needed to talk to you all. Asked me where you lived and I told him; hope that was all right."

"But of course. Odd though, that he would want to talk to us. Probably just—" Mary Adams stopped in mid-sentence. She was interrupted by the sound of her husband's laughter. "What, may I ask, is so funny?"

John Adams couldn't answer. He was too busy giggling to speak. The best he could do was point. When Doc Wilson and Mother followed the line of his finger, they saw what was so funny. Joey was trying to carry Doc's bag. It looked as though he'd dragged it the first ten to twelve feet, then come to the realization that this wasn't going to work. Now, he was kind of crawling underneath it. He had one hand gripping the end of the bag with the other arm out, sort of lifting it onto his back. Then he backed into it, like a hermit crab testing out a new shell. When this didn't work, he tried to turn over and the whole bag fell on top of him. Determined, he slid out from underneath and went to the back of the sack and tried pushing it. He tried rolling it. He tried pulling it again. Finally, he just sat down and leaned against it.

Doc Wilson had to put down his plate and glass, so he wouldn't drop them, as he too began to snicker. After a moment, he composed himself and walked toward the little boy and the big bag.

"Let me get that, Joey," Doc offered. He hoisted the bag and carried it into the living room. Joey followed.

"What in the world have you got in there, Doc?" Father chortled.

"Actually, it's a collection of things," he replied as he reached into the satchel. From inside, he pulled out what looked like a wooden box. As Doc moved it, Joey could hear it make a sort of rattling sound.

"What is it?" the little boy asked excitedly.

"It is a Chinese marble maze. You see those little knobs on the side? Well, they swivel and maneuver the face of the box. Take the marble from inside. It should be in that little slot on the side there," Doc said as he handed the box to Joey. "Now put the marble at the beginning of the maze; the object is to try and make it to the end, without falling into any of the holes that are scattered along the path. If you do go into one of the holes, the marble will roll into the side slot again and you can start over. You understand, Joey?"

"Yeah! Can I try it?"

"You can try it and keep it. I want you to have it. I'm too old for the frustration any more."

"Gosh! Thanks, Doc." With that, the eager youth hurried off to test his skill.

Doc turned his attention back to the parents.

"I wanted to bring by a couple of books. They're about dealing with the loss of a loved one. Joey seemed pretty shook up. Although he does appear to be doing much better now, I get the feeling that he might just be keeping it to himself."

"He's a very considerate little boy," Mother praised. "He doesn't want his unhappiness to make anyone else feel bad."

"I sensed that," Doc replied. "That's why I brought the distraction."

"We appreciate that, Doc, and the books, too," Father said as he patted Doc on the shoulder.

"There are also some clothes, cookware, and other necessities in here. I thought maybe with the mill closing and everything, that you might be able to find someone who could use them. Mr. Brandon's lawyer wanted me to bring a couple of things from the house. I told him I was going to drop some stuff by, and he handed me this bag with a couple of things in it," Doc explained, holding up the Santa sack. "He said they were for Joey. He felt that Nicholas would want him to have them."

Mother and Father pulled all of the goodwill items from the bag, and then peered inside at the small articles that remained. They looked at each other, looked back into the bag, then at Joey.

As they closed the sack, each wiped a tear from their cheek.

Doc finished his pie and eggnog, wished everyone a happy holiday, and said his good-byes. As he left the room, he turned and took one last look. He saw Joey concentrating on his new challenge. He saw John and Mary Adams slip a Christmas kiss and then step into place beside their precious little boy. He saw the rest of the guests and smiled at their smiles. He couldn't help but think that even through the tragedy, they would all look back on this Christmas with fond memories. He knew that sometimes it takes true adversity to make true progress; that out of great sadness comes great happiness; and that in order to completely appreciate the good times, you must first experience the pain and trials of the bad times. "God bless you all," he said to himself as the door closed behind him.

"Dad! Look!" Joey exclaimed as his father peered down over Mom's shoulder. "I made it half way."

"Nice going, Joe," praised father. "You're a natural."

"Shoot! It went in the hole."

"Better luck next time, son."

"Hey, what was in the bag?" Joey asked as he noticed the near empty Santa Claus satchel on the floor next to his parents.

"I was wondering when you were going to get around to that," Mother said with a half giggle. "There were some clothes, some pots and pans, a few knick-knacks, and a couple of things for you from Nicholas."

"From Nicholas? How could I get something from Nicholas?"

"His lawyer said that he wanted you to have them, so he gave them to Doc Wilson to bring over."

"What is it?" Joey wondered aloud.

"Look and see," Father suggested. "He said you could even have the bag."

In seconds the small boy was hovering over the huge sack. Suddenly he stopped. *What could it be?* he wondered. What could Nicholas have wanted him to have? Slowly he opened the big red bag and curiously he peeked inside. It was dark in there. He couldn't really tell what it was. He reached his arm into the inner recesses of the meshed container and pulled out a beautifully engraved gold picture frame. It appeared to be made of solid gold and had flower patterns

Ross Adams

etched into it. The leaves were imbedded with emeralds and the petals were ruby. Each flower was traced with little diamond specks. It was awesome. The detail, the precision, the brilliance of the gems, it was absolutely priceless. Joey admired its beauty, but he knew that it was only metal and rocks. The content of that frame, however, was a moment stolen from time. It was a picture of Nicholas and Caesar on one of their morning treks across the tundra behind the big house. Nicholas looked much younger and Caesar was much smaller. It even gave the impression that the man was walking the dog instead of the other way around. This was much more than paper with well placed colors. It was a remembrance of something and someone that couldn't be made vibrant again with a little polish and some elbow grease. It took thought and emotion, a little imagination, and whole lot of youthful ambition to make the life inside that expensive frame vivid and lasting.

"Look Caesar, it's you," Joey proclaimed as he shoved the photo in front of the dog's nose. "See how little you were then?"

"Is that everything?" Father questioned purposefully.

"I don't know," Joey responded, somewhat surprised by the fact that there could actually be more.

Back into the bag he went, until his entire head and shoulders were lost inside. When his face reappeared, it surrendered a bittersweet smile. For in one hand he held the purple satin box that had sat on the mantle of life in Nicholas's den. Inside the box, was the shiny gold coin he'd put so much passion into restoring. In the other hand was the carefully etched placard he'd given as his greatest present ever. A wave of emotion washed over him like the water that pounded the rocks at Bastion Bay.

"I'm going to my room to put these away." Joey fought back the tears that he knew were on the way. He gathered his things and scampered up the stairs with Caesar at his heels.

The door to Joey's room flew open and made a loud "smack" as it hit the doorstop. The little boy and the dog stumbled into the room and Joey flung himself onto the bed. The joy, the sadness, the love, the anger, the loneliness, the confusion, and the desire to make it all go away, these were the conglomerate feelings that created the initial smile and resulted in the ensuing breakdown of one little boy's emotional psyche. No matter how hard he tried, he couldn't find the solutions to the burning questions and doubts that flooded his brain. If only he could just make it make sense. That seemed a very unlikely scenario as the tears began to flow. Like it often does, crying turned into sleep and sleep to rest. It was a welcome escape.

Downstairs, everyone was getting ready to leave. Mom and Dad were standing at the door, kissing, crying, laughing, and hugging as each guest passed. Eventually, only Uncle Frank and Auntie Alice were left.

"Well, let's get to work," announced Alice. "The party's over. Time to work on cleaning up the mess we all enjoyed so much making."

"You don't have to do that. We can take care of it," Mother stated confidently. Even though she was sure it would do her no good. "You are our guests."

"The exact reason I'm going to do the cleaning. You did all the work putting this together, so the least I can do is get it cleaned up," responded Alice.

"Not by yourself you're not," declared Mother.

No one was sure how long it had taken. It was long enough for Frank to have another piece of pie and fall asleep on the couch, which considering his condition didn't seem all that unfair. But as for the legal measurement of time, it was uncertain. The minutes and hours had evolved into teamwork and fellowship. The actual chore of cleaning the house had become secondary. The fact that it was over was a disappointment as opposed to a cause for celebration. Frank woke as Alice kissed his cheek.

"Honey, wake up. It's time to go, dear"

"I wasn't asleep," Frank said with a sarcastic grin. "Did you think I was sleeping? Nahh. I was just resting my eyes." He laughed.

Frank and Alice said their good-byes and headed for home. As they reached the front walk, they saw a tall man in a dark suit approaching. He was carrying a briefcase.

"Merry Christmas, Mr. Williams," Frank said as they passed.

"A beautiful night for a walk, isn't it? Merry Christmas to you."

Inside the house, John and Mary Adams were finishing up the last of the dinner dishes when the doorbell rang.

"I wonder who that could be."

"Maybe Frank and Alice forgot something."

John grabbed Mary's hand as they walked into the living room.

"I'll get the door, dear. Why don't you go check on Joe?" he offered.

"Good idea."

Father headed to the entrance, while mother made her way upstairs. He opened the door quickly, expecting to see Frank and Alice standing there. Instead, he saw the tall man with the briefcase.

"Hello. May I help you?"

"Good evening, Mr. Adams. My name Is Erik Williams." Erik paused for a moment, waiting for some sign of recognition. Seeing none, he continued. "I am the attorney for Mr. Nicholas Brandon."

"Oh! Yes. How are you? Come on in. We were told you might be coming by."

"Doc Wilson, I presume?"

"Yep. So what can we do for you Mr. Williams?"

"Erik. Please."

"Very well then. What can we do for you Erik Please." Father laughed. Erik laughed as well.

John Adams had a knack for making uncomfortable situations less uncomfortable. He'd done it again.

"Is your wife at home?" Erik asked.

"She just went upstairs to check on our son. It's been a pretty rough day for him."

"I would imagine. Did he get the things I sent over?"

"He sure did. Thank you. I'm sure that when he gets older, he'll have an even greater appreciation for them. Right now, everything is pretty mixed up."

"I'm sure that's true, as well. Now, to answer your question. I am here on behalf of Nicholas. As you know he and your son, Joey, developed quite a friendship in the last few days."

"Yes. It was really very amazing. Nicholas seemed to be all Joe could talk about this week."

"Well, for your information, the same could be said for Mr. Brandon. I'm not sure what it was, but whatever it was, it was special. Anyway, getting to the point, Nicholas called me four days ago and said he wished to change some items in his will. Over the last three days, I have met with him and had discussions over the phone. I'm not sure that you can really understand all of this without having known Nicholas. He is one of the most gracious and kind people that God ever put on this earth. He was quite traumatized by his wife's death and sort of became a hermit in the years since. But make no mistake about it; his heart for people didn't change. I think that may be what drew him to your son. From what I understand, Joey was the one person who may have had an even greater gift for generosity than Nicholas."

"That would not surprise me," the father beamed. "I never met Nicholas, but I know my son. I have never met anyone like him. I would suspect you're right; it would make sense that they were kindred spirits of some kind. The Lord does work in mysterious ways."

"Amen, Mr. Adams. Amen."

"John. Please."

"Okay then. Amen, John Please." Both men burst into laughter and didn't stop until Mother and Joey entered from the stairwell.

"Are we missing something?" Mother asked pleasantly.

"Dear, I would like you to meet Erik Williams, Please." Both the men chuckled again as Father finished. "He's Nicholas Brandon's lawyer."

"Hey, I saw you before," Joey piped in. "You were at Nicholas's house when I came over one day."

"That would have been me," Erik admitted. "And you must be Joey. I've heard a lot of wonderful things about you. As a matter of fact, you're the reason I'm here."

"Me? What did I do?" Joey questioned.

"You made friends with an old man who was in desperate need of someone like you."

"He made friends with me, too," Joey replied.

In the mean time, Caesar had found Erik and was licking his hand.

"Erik, would you like something to drink? I believe there might be some eggnog left. I'd be glad to warm some up for you," offered Mother.

"That would be wonderful. Thank you."

"Why don't we take this into the living room and get comfortable," suggested Dad.

The living room always made things more comfortable for some reason. Joey wasn't sure exactly what it was. He suspected that the fire in the fireplace, the candles on the window sill, and soft carpet on the floor probably had something to do with that warm feeling he felt inside every time the family gathered there.

"What a beautiful tree!" commented Erik.

"I put the angel on top. Dad lifted me up on his shoulders. My Grandma made it," Joey explained enthusiastically.

"It's very pretty. Your Grandma has quite a talent."

"Actually, she's dead now."

"I'm so sorry."

"It's okay. It happened a long time ago, before I was born. So I don't remember it."

The conversation was getting awkward, and Erik couldn't have been happier to hear Mary Adams's voice.

"Here you are, Erik. I hope you like cinnamon."

"I do indeed," was his relieved reply.

Mom handed their guest his drink as Father entered from the dining room. They both sat down in the loveseat. Erik seated himself in the center of the couch. Joey sat on the floor. Erik laid his briefcase in the center of the coffee table and opened it. He then pulled a huge stack of papers from inside. Next, he took a big drink of eggnog and then he spoke.

"Let me just start by saying that Nicholas was a constant giver. As I said before, he was an extremely generous person. He, however, never took credit for any of the things he did. He always demanded anonymity." Noticing the look on Joey's face, Erik simplified, "That means he didn't want anyone to know what he did."

"How come?" Joey asked.

"Because it wasn't important who did it, Joey. The important thing was that he was helping people just like you helped him by polishing that gold coin," Erik explained.

"Oh!" Joey nodded with understanding.

"Nicholas believed that his reason for being here was to make things better. He did it the only way he knew how. Whether it was paying for the Christmas tree in town square or covering past due bills at the generalstore. As you know, Joey, he loved Christmas, because he felt the joy of giving in others as well. So it seems only right that I be here on Christmas evening to tell you about his greatest gift of all—his life. He knew he was dying, but he was never really able to find a purpose for his death. That is, until he met Joey. Having a true friend and hearing the stories of your lives gave him a way to make his death meaningful. That's when he called me. The other thing you may not have understood about him was how stubborn he could be. Once he made up his mind, there was no changing it. So I just listened and wrote it all down in legalese. I would spend hours explaining it, if I was to read you what I wrote. So I'm just going to summarize, and if you have questions, please feel free to ask. I have just finished the paperwork for the deed to the mill where you work, John. Nicholas purchased it, and I have made plans for all the new equipment needed to be obtained. What's more, you will be designated as its primary stock holder and president, with all remaining shares distributed evenly to employees and their families. I have arranged for you to meet with people who can help you get accustomed to your new role, and I am always available to you if you need me. We can discuss this in greater detail later. The next order of business is the medical expenses for your friend, Frank. They are paid in full. There will also be a Christmas bonus for each mill employee to help them get through the holiday. Pay will continue until all repairs and modifications are complete, at which point a profit-sharing pay scale will be established. A large donation has been made to the town as well."

John Adams was dumbfounded. There were no words to describe his emotion. The tears rolling down his wife's cheeks and the ones welling in his eyes were the greatest expression of astonishment and gratitude that either of them could convey. The modest phrase "Thank you" escaped from their mouths amidst the overwhelming awe of the circumstances.

"You are welcome. It is you who are to be thanked. Your lives gave meaning to Nicholas's death, and I thank you on his behalf." Erik now turned to Joey, who appeared to be pretty much taking everything in stride. "The rest of this is about you, Joey."

"Neat." It wasn't much, but it certainly described the young boy's sentiment.

"Nicholas wished for you to take care of Caesar," Erik continued.

"Can Caesar live with us Mom and Dad? Please! Please!" Joey pleaded.

The question need not even be asked, John and Mary thought as they nodded their approval.

"Yippee! Did you here that, boy?" Joey shrieked as he wrapped his arms around his new roommate's neck. "You get to live with us." John

Adams could have sworn he saw the dog winking at him again while licking the boy's face.

"A trust fund has been established in Joey's name to pay for all schooling and other such life necessities. Do you know what that means, Joey?"

"Yeah. Well, kinda. Actually, no. I know that means I'm supposed to go to college."

"It means that when you do go to college, it will be paid for, as well as anything else you might need to succeed."

"Neat." Again, short and to the point.

"Nicholas also wanted you to decide what to do with his house. He said that you would know the right thing to do. I guess that means that you can live there if you want to, or sell it, or something else."

"You said Nicholas didn't want anyone to know about all of the nice things he did for everybody, right?"

"Yes, that is correct."

"Well, does that mean that nobody else can say what he did and how nice he was?"

"No. I don't think that's what it means at all. Nicholas is gone, and I think people should know how nice he was," Erik responded.

"Good. 'Cause I think that, too. I think that we should make his house and everything a memory of him."

"A museum maybe," Father suggested.

"But we have to let Caesar take his walks there," Joey added.

"Certainly," agreed the lawyer. "Perhaps a museum and wildlife park."

"Yeah, and we could put up signs that said all the nice things he did," Joey added.

"An excellent idea, Joey. Nicholas was correct. You did know what to do. I shall put the wheels in motion immediately." Erik smiled and shook his head in wonder. "The will covers a variety of other details, but I think we have taken care of everything concerning your family. I do thank you for your time. I hope you are as pleased with the outcome as I am. I truly believe that this is what Nicholas wanted as well." At this point, he gathered all his papers and placed them back into his case. He closed it and locked it, then took another gulp of eggnog and stood up. "It has indeed been a Christmas to remember. I don't think anything in our little town will ever be quite the same. A change for the better, I believe. John and Mary, thank you again for your hospitality and kindness. It is easy to see where your son gets it." Erik walked over to Joey, got down on one knee, and looked him squarely in the eye. "Joey, it has been an honor to meet you. You are a very special person. Don't let the world change you. If you will just continue to be true to yourself and who God made you to be, you can change the world, just like you changed it this Christmas." Erik stood and shook Joey's hand, then patted Caesar's head and started for the front door.

"Erik." Father's voice stopped him. "Thank you," he said as he rushed to get the door.

"My pleasure. Goodnight. God bless, and Merry Christmas." That said, the tall man with the briefcase exited and disappeared into the dark.

Caesar walked over to Joey and licked his hand. Joey scratched behind his ears and kissed his nose. Father walked over to Mother and hugged her. Mother kissed his lips. Something was different. Joey didn't know what it was, but that emptiness and confusion deep inside him had somehow been taken away. He felt good. He felt great actually. Erik was right. It had been a Christmas to remember.

"Mom, can I have another piece of pumpkin pie?"

"Yes, you may, son. Then it's time to get ready for bed."

Joey went to the kitchen and helped himself to the largest slice of pie he could find. He grabbed a fork from the drawer and a glass from the cupboard. He put the pie and the fork on the kitchen table, then went to the refrigerator and poured himself some milk. He carried the milk back to the table and sat down to eat.

In the living room, Mother and Father were tidying up and still trying to take in what had just happened.

"See, I told you that the Lord has a way of taking care of things." Mother laughed.

"He certainly does," Father replied. "And you were right about not understanding it. But then again, who are we to try and make sense of God's miracles."

"We're not. We're just here to appreciate them. By the way, I think you'll make a great businessman."

"I only wish I had your confidence."

"Look, you were a great foreman. You're a great father. You're a great husband. You're a great person, dear. There is no reason to think you won't be a great president for the mill. Erik said he would help and that he would get you all the backing you need. You'll be fine."

"Thank you, sweetheart. I'm sure you're right. With your support and the help of all of my friends, old and new, this should be a piece of cake," Father concluded, still not completely convinced but feeling much better just the same.

Joey was just finishing his glass of milk when Mom and Dad came into the kitchen.

"Well, Joe. How was that pie?" Father inquired.

"It was delicious. I had a really big piece, and I ate it all," bragged Joey.

"Good for you, dear. Now wash that plate and glass and then head upstairs and brush your teeth. When you're done with that, get your pajamas on and get in bed. Dad and I will be up in a bit to tuck you in."

"Okay, Mom." Joey carried his dishes to the sink and washed them. He put everything into the drain rack and then bounded up the stairs to the bathroom.

Mother put the last of the dishes away, while Dad put the pie in the pie rack and wiped the counters.

Teeth brushed, face washed, pajamas on, Joey was peeling back the covers on his bed. Something was strange. The blankets felt extraordinarily heavy. He lifted the flap and looked, then put the bedding back the way he'd found it. Sitting on the bed were the priceless picture and frame, the purple box, and the engraved piece of wood. Joey reached down and picked them up. He looked at them for a long time. Then his face contorted. Not into the sad puckered face he would have expected but instead into a full-fledged smile. He placed the items on the nightstand. He pulled the knitted afghan from the foot of the bed and spread it out on the floor.

"Here's your bed, Caesar, right next to me," he said.

As he slipped into bed and pulled the covers up to his chin, his parents walked in.

"Well, son, it's been quite a day, hasn't it?" announced Father.

"Yep, Dad, it has."

"Is there anything that you want to ask Mom or me before we go back downstairs?'

"Nope. I think I just need to sleep. I'm tired."

"As well you should be, little man. As well you should. I won't read you a story tonight then, instead I will just quote one simple verse. One I'm sure you have memorized. 'For God so loved the world that he gave his only begotten Son, and whosoever believeth in him, shall not perish but have everlasting life.' What verse is that, Joe?"

"John 3:16."

"That's right, sport. Now you get some rest."

"I will, Dad."

"We love you very much, sweetie. We are so proud of you. You have done more than you can possibly understand." Mother was near tears again as she added, "Sleep tight, honey."

"Okay, Mom. I love you, too."

Mary and John Adams each kissed their little blessing from God on the forehead. They turned and walked out of the room, taking time to pet Caesar on the way by.

"I love you, Caesar," the little boy said as he reached down and hugged the dog's neck. Caesar licked Joey's cheek and made himself comfortable in his new bed.

Joey looked at the nightstand and the items that garnished it. He smiled again and said his prayers.

"Dear Jesus, I know I'm only a little boy, but I think I'm starting to understand why you were born. You were brought to earth to save people like me and my friends and family. That is why you are called our Savior. To be able to really help all the people on earth, you had to die. And now I understand why Nicholas had to die, too. 'Cause he was like you; he was on earth to make life better for people, too. And the best way that he could help us was to die. I'm not real crazy about all this dying stuff, but I think that sometimes that's just God's plan. When we've done all we can do for him here, we have to move on and let things be better without us. I'm really glad I got to be Nicholas's friend. I'm glad that he was my friend, too. I also think this has been the best Christmas ever. Thank you for being born and for dying for us. God bless Mommy and Daddy and Grandma and Grandpa and all of my family and friends. Thank you, God, for Jesus and for Nicholas. AMEN."

e|LIVE

listen|imagine|view|experience

AUDIO BOOK DOWNLOAD INCLUDED WITH THIS BOOK!

In your hands you hold a complete digital entertainment package. In addition to the paper version, you receive a free download of the audio version of this book. Simply use the code listed below when visiting our website. Once downloaded to your computer, you can listen to the book through your computer's speakers, burn it to an audio CD or save the file to your portable music device (such as Apple's popular iPod) and listen on the go!

How to get your free audio book digital download:

1. Visit www.tatepublishing.com and click on the e|LIVE logo on the home page.
2. Enter the following coupon code:
   dec0-43dc-7add-a278-0e35-4828-04dd-96d4
3. Download the audio book from your e|LIVE digital locker and begin enjoying your new digital entertainment package today!